T0365056

The Fallen Series

Book 1 Fallen

Megan D. Harding

authorHOUSE®

AuthorHouse™
1663 Liberty Drive
Bloomington, IN 47403
www.authorhouse.com
Phone: 1 (800) 839-8640

Published by AuthorHouse 11/29/2016

ISBN: 978-1-5246-5220-3 (sc)
ISBN: 978-1-5246-5219-7 (e)

Print information available on the last page.

This book is printed on acid-free paper.

Preface

Love doesn't always have a happy ending and things are never as they seem. It would be easy to look around and just see the world as it is. To only see everyday life filled with work, family and friends. What if there was more? Something beyond what we can see with our naked eye? What if there were angels roaming above our heads and demons snickering at our every move? Is that not what we were told when we were younger? Loved ones go to Heaven to become angels that watch over us, and if there are angels wouldn't there be demons lurking around every corner waiting to trap and attack? The truth is- there are.

Angels aren't necessarily cute baby cupids flying around in those ridiculous diapers. On the contrary, angels are uncommonly large, and often beautifully terrifying, with wings that can take the form of many different materials. If in battle, their wings may turn into a metal to become armor. If an angel takes the form of a human as an attempt to blend in, their wings do not disappear, but become like air so that they do not take up any space around them.

Angels are quite organized and, like humans, have many jobs. The first and most important angels are the seven Archangels. Their position can never be filled nor replaced by any living or spiritual being. With impenetrable armor and double-edged swords with the Word of God imprinted on them, they keep the law of the kingdom in order and free of any imperfections. They are: Michael, Gabriel, Raphael, Uriel, Selaphiel, Raguel, and Barachiel. They each have different abilities such as healing, preserving nature and balance, prophesy, helping people cross over at the time of death, and other spiritual gifts.

You also have the messenger angels. They are the angels that send prayers from the people to God. They are angels of few words, yet take joy in bringing back news from the Father and never miss anything. Messenger angels are quite small, but extremely fast. It is said that when someone randomly feels dizzy or gets a sense of Deja vu, it is because a messenger just passed by.

Next are the Angels of praise. They are all encompassed by light and sing praises to the Father day and night. Peace and joy flows through them always. They flock to those who feel like they are in the dark. They cannot change a person's mood or mindset, but they can spread light on any joyful areas in a person's life in hopes that they will turn their sorrows to joy and praise.

Last, you have the Guardians- the largest group of angels. They are broken into groups spread around regions of the world and reside in "Sanctuaries", large unoccupied buildings that are disguised and camouflaged so that humans cannot enter them. If humans go near a sanctuary they start to feel a deep compelling sensation to want to leave. Guardians are specifically assigned to their mission, which are the people the Father designated them to protect. Messengers have the authority to send guardians to a human, or free-will as some angels call them, in absolute need. Guardians are large, glorious, and scary beings who wield knives and swords with God's word written upon it. When a guardian is assigned to a person or family, they become their 'mission' opposed to calling them humans. Guardians can guide, heal, and protect their missions.

Demons are not much different than the angels. There are two types of demons. The first are the Fallen. They were once angels that fell from grace. Their wings were stripped from them, and they were forced to work with Lucifer, the Devil. The Fallen are broken into two groups. The first is the group that came down with Lucifer in the beginning, then there are the ones that have fallen from grace since. They look very similar to the Guardians, but they have massive scars down their backs where they once had wings.

The second type of demons are the damned. They are people who have sold their souls to Lucifer. After an unconceivable amount of torture, some are trusted and used as pawns to do the dirty work on Earth. Their numbers seem to increase by the second with the help of vampires and sometimes werewolves.

Every twenty-five years there is an event called the Quarterly Sweep. This strategic battle between beings of the light and creatures of the dark is to hash out rules and areas of domain for the Guardians and the Fallen. This accordance keeps balance to prevent one side from out numbering the other. In the meantime, the tension of these two worlds is immensely and extremely high.

And so the story begins…

There are many sects of Guardians around the world. The leader of the Guardians in this particular sect is Idris. She is a strong and mighty being, yet gentle and wise. She is able to speak directly to the Father- as can all guardians, but as head guardian she requires a great deal of communication. There are many high ranking guardian leaders who are in charge of different things. One of the most powerful guardians is Abner.

He began his training early on to take Idris's place if anything were to happen to her. Guardians often transform to manifest in human form and blend in with the people around them. They call it cloaking. When they appear in angel form they are invisible to the naked eye. Abner cloaked many times which lead to him taking a young woman and sleeping with her. He conceived a child within her. The Father knew what Abner had done. He had defiled a human and was now being drained of his glorious power. Abner hid Catharine until she was able to have the baby.

A few guardians went looking for Abner, but were never seen again. When two more guardians went looking for answers it was revealed that a small battle had taken place in a safe house where Abner kept Catharine. The first two guardians who were dispatched to the safe house were slaughtered, along with a few fallen. The devastation hit when they realized that young Catherine was also gruesomely slaughtered with her belly ripped open.

At first, it seemed that the child was nowhere to be found. One day soon after the horrific events, Idris flew back to the sanctuary holding a small baby. He wasn't like any human baby that has ever lived. His hair radiated a golden blond and his eyes were a deep piercing blue. He was much larger than any baby that would look to be at his age, and the baby had what looked like nubs on his back that might one day become wings. This was the Nephilim child. Idris explained that he would be raised in the sanctuary as a guardian, for she was told of a prophesy that the young Nephilim must fulfill.

Chapter 1

ALANA

The sins of the father *fall* to the son. This sounds like something that was once drilled into my head at Sunday School, told to children to scare them from sin. The same idea as Santa Claus, I suppose. You better watch out, you better not pout, because Santa Claus is coming to town. Parents tell their children to be good so they can get presents, but if they are bad they get coal.

Why coal, I wonder? Maybe that is the difference between presents and coal. Presents mean life, but coal is cold, hard, and black. Someone is always watching, they would say. Although no one ever seems to know who *they* are. I have always been curious about such things. About death, about life. How could you just be either or? Could there be more than eyes open and eyes closed? It seems morbid to think of death at such a young age.

It's the same thing every day. White walls, tiny desks, notebooks, and the professor. College. Where life begins. Some say life begins at birth. Or was life always there? Like in math when we learn about a line. It never begins or ends. Its infinity and beyond, or is that just a line from some children's movie?

I need to focus. I'm supposed to write something about myself. An introductory paragraph. I hate when professors make students do this. What is it exactly that they want to know? Either your life is boring and you don't know what to put down, or your life is completely complicated and don't have enough room to write everything down.

I guess I could start by saying, hi, I'm Alana. I'm 19 years old, or young. I guess I should say young. I don't always feel young. On the outside, I'm smart, funny, spunky, a cheerleader. Or, at least, I was in high school. My mom always wanted me to be a cheerleader like her. I don't cheer anymore, it's not my thing. Not that I'm not cheerful. I just have a lot going on with school and life. That seems like something a grown up would say.

Focused is what most people say about me. Now I spend most of my time studying or at church. Yes, I'm a Christian, that's probably social suicide at a college university. Although, I seem to be having no problem making friends.

I left home to attend Sam Houston State University. I was planning on going to community college at Lamar like most of my friends, but my grandmother has been trying to persuade me to leave home and "find myself". She always says I take on too much responsibility. I know she just wants what's best for me, but the past few years have been hard. Especially since Papa Joe has been getting worse. Neither of them talk about it. I'm not even quite sure what's wrong, but I've noticed. I see things. I've seen how a lively, fun grandfather can start to slip away. He's lost so much, so I don't blame him. Although, it's more than that. His health is declining. He barely laughs anymore. I can tell he is trying to stay strong for me. Grandma Hazel would never knowingly place any more burdens on me, so she just says he's getting old and that he's tired. I don't know how they convinced me to move almost two hours away. I still visit most weekends, but lately I've been so busy. Now I'm starting my second year of college, while trying desperately to maintain my 4.0 G.P.A

What is it exactly that my professor wants to know about his students? My name is Alana. I wonder, does our name shape our personalities, or does our personality shape our name. Our names are given at, or before birth, so I think I'd agree with the first statement. My name means light, at least that's what my mom would always tell me. I was the light of her world. Was. I can't think about that right now. *Was* doesn't define me. What does define a person?

My favorite color is blue. But not powder blue like your grandmother wears, and not primary color blue that decorates little boy's room. I like teals and turquoises, like the ocean. The ocean has always been my favorite place. It can be so peaceful, yet it's so large, like infinity. It has a beginning, but doesn't seem to ever end. Some things end though.

Class is almost over and I still don't know what to write. The quote on the poster "The sins of the father fall to the son." What does that have to do with an English class? It's not even inspirational. Unless, perhaps, it is supposed to encourage me to be the best I can be. Instead it just seems discouraging. Like there is nothing you can do. What's done is done.

The professor, doctor something hard to pronounce that I will never get right, stepped in front of the class and said pencils down in a terribly monotone voice. He must have heard that a lot growing up from his teachers because looking around, everyone used pens.

I looked over my introductory page. It seemed decent enough. I wrote that I was once a cheerleader, I wrote about my favorite color, and that I want to be a Doctor. I couldn't help but to write about my dog Bucky, even though he still lives at home. I wish I was permitted to bring him to our dorm rooms. I even mentioned my best friend Alexis who I have known forever. We have always been best friends. Although, we are mostly opposites. I'm surprised we're so close with her being, well, Lexi.

She has been trying to convince me to go to this huge party all week.

It seemed like there was always a huge party, of the century, that she just couldn't miss or she would die. The one this weekend was no different. I just moved back to the dorms a couple of weeks ago and class just started on Monday. The first part of the week is easy. The monotone reading of all the syllabi that seem to say the exact same thing in every single class, every single year. Now we have moved on to the 'Fun, get to know each other phase'. That only means that the real work is coming soon. I don't mind it though, I like a challenge. Although, a part of me is already eager to get out of here. Yet, there's a part of me that never wants to leave.

I don't really like to party. I'm more of a hang out at a local coffee shop girl. I like to listen to local bands and study, while slowly slipping into a coffee coma. That's what Lexi calls it. I'm pretty immune to coffee, although after my fifth cup I can practically act drunk and maybe even climb walls. Like I said, I can be pretty calm and serious... But I do have my spunky side.

Lexi on the other hand, is full of spunk! She's, as we say in the south, something else. To be honest, I thought she was really weird at first. She doesn't seem to ever be down to Earth. All she cares about is boys. And man is it awkward when I open my door and come face to face with whoever her new boy is.

Lexi sort of comes from the perfect family. Her dad is super rich and her mom is fabulously beautiful. They have been married something like twenty five years, but Lexi is an only child. She's used to getting what she wants. She learned that from her mom because her dad 'screws up' a lot, or around is more like it. I guess maybe they aren't the 'perfect family'. I'm not too sure Lexi is here for an education, not saying she isn't absolutely brilliant. I would choose her as a study partner any day, well if she would actually show up to study. And since she is so used to getting what she wants, she has maniacally tricked me into going to some frat party. Although, I'm basically her DD (designated driver). Show up, pretend to have a good time, and keep her out of trouble, well too much trouble.

It's not that I don't like to have fun, it's just that I have a goal. I want to help people. I want to be a doctor, and that is going to require a lot of school. I don't have time to fail a class. I certainly don't have time to get tangled up with some frat boy with no real ambitions. This is my third semester at college. Since I took the dual credit college classes offered at our high school, and I have taken some summer school and extra classes I'm technically a junior. I plan to graduate early with honors and be accepted into medical school.

I'm sure I will still be around Lexi. She's practically my sister. She's been my best friend for as long as I have known her. She's been there for me when I needed her most. We have talked about the different medical schools that I might get accepted into and she normally brings up different ideas than mine. Like how much she would love to move to a big city and try to pursue music, or art, or some rich guy. Whichever is more fun, she says. She's kind of a wild flower. One with no real roots. Much like a dandelion, she can spread her joy and love of life with anyone around her. I needed that at one point. She says I am her roots. I guess like a tree, I keep her rooted, but she is like the sun and helps me grow. I feel more like a baby sitter sometimes. Tonight is one of those occasions.

"Oh God Alana! You're not wearing that. Please tell me you are not wear that tonight!" Lexi gasped as the door flew open and she fluttered in.

It's August, in Texas, so I wore something comfortable to class, but also cute and professional so I can make a good impression my first couple of weeks at school. As I peered down, I was wearing white high wasted shorts that came down mid-thigh, and a silk polka-dot button up blue blouse with a collar, and some flats. My hair has always been really long and I managed to curl it, but it ended up in a low ponytail to the side. She hates when I wear a pony tail. I got my red hair from my grandmother, but hers is mostly gone now. Some parts of it still remain. I like to look back at picture of her and imagine what she must have been like at my age.

Lexi always explains that I dress like a prep school girl, but not the sexy kind. She says that I not only look like my grandmother, but I dress like her too. I would giggle every time she would mention me being sexy.

"In your dreams." I would normally reply.

Of course, she was wearing skin tight holey jeans, a tank top, and sparkly boots. Her blond hair was perfect, despite the Texas heat and humidity. It felt like you were walking into a water park the moment you put one foot out the door. After I gave her my very puzzled, yet completely innocent look she pointed me to the closet. No words. Just one hand on her hip and the other pointed at the closet door. I caught her about to say something like "You can borrow some of my clothes". But, I put my hand out to shut her up. There is no way I could fit into anything she owned. And if I did, I have no idea how I would walk or bend. It's a talent I guess.

There is no winning with Lexi. I slowly dragged myself to my closet with a pitiful pouty face. She couldn't hold in her smile. Her smile was almost contradictory. She seemed genuine and mischievous at the same time. She just shook her head and gave me the "what am I going to do with you" look she always gives me.

In the back of my closet I found a cute white church dress. It was sleeveless, came up to my collar bone in the front, and down to my knees. Although, it did have a lacy peekaboo back. I let my hair down and threw on some sandals and a summery blue cardigan that wasn't too hot to wear. When I felt her going to insist I lose the jacket, I gave her a look and she gave up.

"It wouldn't kill you to show a little, but then again. More for me." She let out with a prissy tone.

I can't believe she talked me into going. Then again, she could talk her way into anything. Or out of anything. We decided to take her car (her Lexus that she named Lexi. After herself of course) because it would 'attract attention'. She would drive there, and if I couldn't keep her out of trouble I would drive us back. As we pulled up to a raging frat house I very much wanted to turn around and go home. Too late. Off she runs. Boy is she fast.

Chapter 2

ALANA

Fantastic. She made it to, and through the door without me. She promised she wouldn't leave me alone. It seemed chilly out, although it wasn't. It was the beginning of September. It was supposed to be fall but the Texas heat still scorched at my skin. I could tell fall was coming. The colors were starting to fade to their warmer colors and even though the heat still simmered around me, I could feel a slight breeze. A promise that summer was coming to an end.

Summer has always been my favorite. Well, spring I guess. I love the warm breezes, the water, and especially the flowers. My grandparents had a lot of land. Not like a ranch or farm, but enough for a garden with flowers everywhere. Both planted and wild. I liked the wild flowers. Bucky liked the flowers too.

Bucky was this little white fur ball I found one day by the house. Really I think he found me. He followed me everywhere. My grandma pretends to hate him, but I know she enjoys his company. He's just a little spunkier than what she would like. I know Papa Joe would prefer a hound dog. Bucky just runs around and eats the flowers in the garden. My favorite spot was a tree that had a swing on it. It was really just a block of wood that my papa Joe made into a swing for my mom when she was really little. It mostly liked the old willow tree by the pond. I was quiet there. Peaceful. As I noticed the slight chill in the air, I began to cross my arms. Honestly, I think it was mostly because I was uncomfortable. I neared the doorstep. Do I just walk in? That's what everyone else did.

The first thing I noticed was the smell. It smelled like college frat boys I guess. Alcohol, pizza rolls, and too many different kinds of musky. The frat house was packed. I definitely felt overdressed when I started looking around. Not like I wore something too fancy, more like everyone around me was wearing less than me, which made me feel uncomfortable. I don't know why. Then I heard her. That laugh. There were many laughs that Lexi had. This one was her flirty laugh. He must be something special to pull it out so quickly.

I glanced around, arms still folded, until I found her. I rushed over stepping over different things. And people. I caught up to her and gave her a look. She knew which one. She hesitatingly giggled and introduced me. Caleb Channing was his name. He was tall dark and handsome. He seemed popular. Just her type. She signaled me. A small scratch of her eye brow with her thumb. No one would notice except me. If I tried to do it every one would notice. I'm not as sly as she is. But, I knew what it meant. It was her silently pleading with me for a little space. I gave her another look, one that should have scared her but I guess I'm as scary as a bunny, and then I walked away.

I was a little thirsty, but wasn't going to dare to drink anything here. It was so loud. I had stashed a book and some study notes in my purse, but Lexi talked me into leaving it in the car. Why did I listen to her? Why did I always listen to her? I tried to walk around for a couple of minutes. Maybe I would recognize someone. I mean, I did have friends. No one here seemed interested in talking about books or biology.

I found a nice enough chair facing outside. The campus is really nice and has a lot of nature. I stared out into the night sky. It was getting late and I just wanted to go home. Well to our dorm room anyways. Lexi's dad made sure we were 'comfortable', so we had the big dorms that looked similar to an apartment. It was small, but we had a shared kitchen and bath, and each had our own room. Although it was just big enough to fit a bed, a desk, and a dresser. But for now, it was home. And that's where I wanted to be.

Lexi can irritate me sometimes, but for some reason tonight I was

getting more and angrier with her. We rode together so I couldn't just drive away. I kept signaling her and trying to get her attention, but she kept ignoring me. She promised she would be by my side. I needed her by my side. Finally I walked up to her and grabbed her arm.

She lashed back and yelled "What's your problem?"

I was stunned. She has never yelled at me before. I stared at her with big doe eyes. I was shocked. Even the boy she was with, looked shocked and confused.

She looked slightly embarrassed, but just looked at me and said "if you want to be a party pooper fine go ahead, but I'm having fun. I'm staying."

"Fine." I replied. "Fine", that's all I had? "Fine"?

That's it. I was ready to go home. I reached for my keys as I walked to the door. After a quick pat down, I remembered that we took her car. She had the keys. I couldn't stand going back to her to ask for her keys. Our dorm wasn't too far away. All the dorms seemed to outline the campus. Although the frat houses were technically 'off-campus', but still within walking distance. 'I'll just walk home.' I thought.

I looked back and couldn't even see her anymore. I headed out the door. The fresh air was nice. Again, I crossed my arms and looked around. I was pretty sure I knew the fastest way home. I saw Lexi's car, stopped, but then passed it up and kept walking.

The moon wasn't quite full, but was bright enough to light the sky. There were plenty of light around so it wasn't completely dark, but still the dark has always bothered me. I tried to stay calm but I felt like I was being watched. I tried to reach into my pocket of my dress to grab my phone, but I must have left it in my purse. The same purse Lexi made me leave in her car. I started to get nervous, but tried calming myself. I began to pray for safety and peace. Then I heard noises.

Chapter 3

LIAM

The Guardian sanctuary looked empty. It was a Saturday night, and Saturday nights were always busy for us guardians. Almost every night was busy. Busy for everyone but me at least. I haven't seen much of Atticus lately. I thought he was finally starting to trust me. Maybe it wasn't him. Maybe it was her. Who was she trying to protect? She's not my mom.

I know how the job works. I might not have been doing it as long as the others, but I've been raised in it my entire life. How can I prove myself if they never give me a chance? I rarely get to leave this abandoned Cathedral.

At least that's what it looks like to human eyes. To us it's the Sanctuary. It's were we receive our orders, where we communicate with others, and, honestly, I suppose it's where we hide. We're not exactly hiding from the fallen ones, they can't come looking for us here. It would break the quarterly accords.

Although, I couldn't tell you where their headquarters are. But we hide, all the same. We hide from our missions, the humans. It seems like everything would be simpler if the humans could see and hear us. But I guess that would defeat faith. We can't interfere, not without approval. I'm not even assigned to a family or person like most Guardians are. I'm the tag a-long. The screw up. I've always been the screw up. I'm not worthy because of who I am. I didn't chose to be half human. They don't even call me by my name most of the time. They just call me Nephilim.

Just then, Baron blew the sanctuary doors open. He seemed to beam with radiance, and maybe a smidge of arrogance. I mean, not arrogance of course. Angels can't be arrogant. He could sure fool me though.

"Hey Nephilim! Busy night?" Hey called out with a smirk.

Alabaster went over to Baron to record the events that took place. Alabaster is a messenger Angel. He rarely talks. When I was a child I used to make funny faces to see if I could distract him. He's probably the most serious Angel I have ever met. And one of the smallest. There is a library in the middle of the sanctuary with recorded events dating back to the beginning of time. I've used it to study, since I haven't been around since the beginning. Although, I want to be out in the world, not in a stupid library. You can only learn so much from books. I want experience.

Baron kept that cheesy grin on his face. He always seemed so proud. Baron likes to be liked. He thinks he's the best. Apparently this time he slowed a car that a teenage boy was driving so that he missed an oncoming car. Our Leader, Idris, walked in. She looked like she had as long as I have remembered her. She had light ebony skin with a hint of rose and her tight curled hair bounces playfully around her soft face. Almost motherly, but her eyes are like stones of golden amber, setting ablaze anything she laid eyes on. She can be very compassionate. Maybe that's why I'm still around. But, she's also very fierce.

I was trained by Atticus. His weapon of choice is a bow and arrow. He likes to distance himself from the fight. Although, I know he was undercover as a soldier in World War 2. Which means he can use a sword, and a gun, but we don't use guns. Our weapons were specially forged with the Word of God written upon them. They are deadly to demons. Wounds from our weapons are nearly impossible for a demon to heal. I'm better with a sword than anything else.

I have one large, broad sword that I keep on my back. My wings, when closed, cover it. I also keep two short blades at my side for a quick draw. I haven't had much opportunity to use any of them though. Mostly I go on missions to clean up messes, or influence missions. We can whisper to them and it can help humans with decisions and actions, but ultimately it's up to them. I always get stuck with whispering. Baron is the go-to angel who deals with the fallen ones.

As Baron walked off he bumped my left shoulder. "Careful Nephilim. You've been so quiet, I barely knew you were there. Slow night, as always?"

That was it. A fire radiated from within me. I needed out. I needed to do something. Now. I have been stuck here too long.

I made my way upstairs to where my resting quarters were. Angels really didn't need rest unless injured in a battle, but I was made to rest every once and a while because of my human side. I knew this building like the back of my hand. When I was younger I would try to sneak out I wanted to see the humans and to know what they were like. I was so curious about who they were and how they lived. How did they not even know about us? I never made if far without Idris knowing I was missing, but she seemed busy tonight. Busy enough so that she wouldn't notice if I took a night run.

I neared the window and opened the clasps. It was one of the old windows that swung out instead of sliding up. It made almost a small door, which was perfect to fit through as a child. It led out to what looked similar to a balcony. I stood there with my eyes closed. I took a deep breath. A small since of disobedience crept over me. I started to have second thoughts, but what's the worst that could happen? I took another deep breath and stepped off the rooftop. I started to fall towards the ground. I heart began to race. I liked to think of it as a game. It was the mist excitement I could find around here. As I neared pavement I opened my wings and glided towards the night sky. Night time was my favorite because it felt so peaceful and so alive at the same time.

I liked the dark. At the sanctuary it seemed like everyone was always looking at me. Growing up Idris had to drag me from place to place to show everyone that the Nephilim child was nothing to fear. I was kept under a spotlight with every move watched, recorded, and related back to higher ranking Angels. I had never heard directly from the Father. That was one thing that separated me from the others. I had to get my orders from them. That's probably why I have never been trusted to be on my own.

I liked it. The feeling that no one was watching me. I was alone.

Chapter 4

Alana

It was dark. The men started to walk towards me. I felt terror resonating through my whole body. I felt as if I couldn't move but for some reason my legs kept going. One leg in front of the other. Eyes staring straight on fiercely as if fixed on a designated target, and that target was me, Alana. One by one they started to crowd me. I couldn't make out faces, they were masked in the darkness. I wanted to count how many there were but I was too terrified to look. It was like my brain and my body were not in sync with each other. One thing I could tell was that there were more than one of them.

"Where do you think you're going?" One of them called out.

I knew I was near campus, but probably not near enough so that anyone could hear me. And if so, no one would be out at this hour.

Without realizing it they had all backed me into a corner. I wasn't sure where I was I was by a building. I could smell the dumpster I was backing into. I felt like such an idiot. How did they manage to get me in a corner? There was nowhere to run. I never go anywhere alone, especially at night. Why had I left the party? Why had I not brought my phone with me? A million thoughts rushed passed my mind but it still seemed as though I couldn't move. This is what people talk about when they say you are scared stiff. What where these men going to do to me? Rob me? I had nothing on me except my mother's necklace and a ring my grandmother had given me with a small cross on it. Neither of which had much value.

What if they didn't want anything from me? What if they wanted me? The thought horrified me and as much as I wanted to fight back, it was like I couldn't. There were at least four or five of them. What could I possibly do? They could do anything they wanted with me. They could leave me for dead and I could maybe get a punch in. I could run, but I'm not very fast. I excelled in academics, not athletics.

I have no idea why, but in that moment I thought of Lexi. How much guilt she would feel about making her friend walk home. And then having something so tragic happen to her best friend. Then my mind went to my grandparents. They couldn't survive losing me too.

"I can't die, I just can't. I don't want to." I kept saying over and over in my head. I need to find a way out of this. I just need to look around. There has to be something I can use. I won't go out without a fight.

Then I saw his eyes. There was something different about them. Something not right. Almost like they were glowing, but they weren't. It was like they could all see me, but all I could see were their eyes. They all had similar eyes. It was all I could see of them. One of them kept slowly coming closer to me. I fell to my knees. He grabbed my arm lightly and lifted me up as if I weighed no more than a set of keys.

Another voice yelled to hurry up. They all started talking and arguing but I couldn't understand what they were saying. I couldn't keep my eyes open. The blood was rushing through my veins. I felt like I was on fire. I could hear my own heart beating so loud like it was screaming for someone to save me. Adrenaline was coursing through my veins, but so was fear.

I felt like I was about to pass out. I saw what looked like a flash of light and a loud thundering noise. The man had let go of me and I fell back to the cold concrete ground. I didn't know what was happening. I was screaming at my body to move. Now was the chance, I just had to move. I gathered the courage and strength as quickly as I could. I couldn't seem to run. All I could do was cower and scoot away behind the dumpster. Why was I being like this? I am a strong woman. I can make a run for it.

I heard the men fighting with someone. I couldn't see much. It was too dark. I thought I kept seeing flashes of light. I couldn't make out who the men for fighting. It was like there was no one there. I didn't understand what I was seeing. Were they dying? How was that possible? I closed my eyes again, then opened them to peek back in the crack between the dumpster and the wall. I saw four bodies. They were lying lifeless on the concrete. It seemed like there was blood everywhere.

Someone else was still here. I could feel it. I thought about getting up and running away or keep hiding. Maybe they didn't know I was there. I had slipped away when he arrived and I hadn't made any noise that I was aware of. I didn't even know how many they were. But if they could take those four or five strong men, then they could take me.

I tried to silence my heavy breathing. My heart was still beating so loud. At first when I wanted it to beat loud in hopes of someone hearing my screaming heart, now I just wished that it would stop. I wanted there to be no evidence of me there. Whoever this was could be dangerous too. I felt him come closer. I opened my eyes but could still see nothing.

Maybe there was something. Something seemed to reflect the moonlight. Had I been crying? Was I looking through my own tears? Then he was just there. It was still really dark but there seemed to be some kind of light from somewhere. Maybe it was the moon light. This couldn't be the same guy who had just killed all of those men. He just stood there staring at me. He had no blood on him. No weapons that I could see. He looked normal. Kind, even. Though I couldn't place the look on his face. He seemed proud of what he had done, but also seemed afraid. Like, afraid of me, or afraid that I saw him. It was like he also looked curious.

He was tall. Much taller than me, but I'm not very tall at all. Most people tower over my petite frame. He had these piercing blue/ green eyes. It was almost like there were bits of gold in his eye. They looked magical. He had this long blond hair that hung above his ears, near his eyes. If it was longer it could have hidden his face. There was something calming about his presence. I seemed to study him in just a few seconds. My eyes followed his broad shoulders to his toned arms. He was wearing a dark shirt and dark pants. He had no cuts, no bruises, and no marks at all. He came closer to me. I saw him reach out to me. It was like he was going to hold me. I kept staring into his eyes. I felt like the entire ocean was in his eyes. Maybe the entire world. He placed one hand behind me and one on my head. I thought he was going to help me up.

Suddenly I felt very calm. I felt a tired and a peace that I have never felt before. My eyes began to close and I began to faint. Everything went black. Everything was silent. There was nothing awake in me. My mind didn't even dream. I awoke to the door slamming suddenly.

"Where have you been? I've been worried sick! What were you thinking? I didn't know where you were? I didn't know if something had happened to you? I'm so sorry I made you leave? Where have you been?" Lexi explained with panic and anger I her voice.

Chapter 5

Liam

Right then I sensed her. A young girl. She was cornered by a group of people. It was probably some drunk party girl. As I got closer, I realized they weren't people. They were demons. Well, a type of demon. People mostly call them vampires. I guess that's really what they are. They are a low level demon who prey on the blood of people. A long time ago when Jesus walked the Earth, Judas his follower betrayed him. He was wrenched with guilt and attempted to end his own life. A curse was laid on him, a personal gift from Lucifer himself. Judas would be granted eternal life to walk the Earth. He would have many followers who would drink of his blood and have many powers as Jesus did. Although, it wasn't the same. When the first people drank of Judas' blood, they hungered for more. They went out to the streets and started hunting people. They have tried to hide what they are. That's why they got their reputation for only being out at night. Most demons look down on vampires. They use them as errand runners. The demons tolerate the vampires, and the vampires do the dirty work and stay protected.

I'm not sure if I wanted to protect her, or if I just wanted to fight. But a fight was about to happen. I descended to the ground. The vampire was holding the girl up. I was sure I had come in time. I wasn't quite sure how many there were. I pulled my sword from behind my wings and ran fearlessly towards the group of vampires. The first one seemed to almost run straight into my sword. Well this will be easy, I thought. The next one wasn't quite so easy. They were strong, and they were fast. I hadn't encountered many vampires before. They didn't have weapons, but they almost didn't need any.

They were faster than anything I had ever seen. Their strength was unfathomable. I almost wasn't sure how to fight them, but I had practiced so much the sword felt like a part of me, like an extension of my arm. I pulled the sword out of him and lunged toward the others. One of them came at me from the side with full force, knocking me off balance loosening the grip on my sword. Another one managed to get the sword knocked out of my hand. I wasn't going to make that mistake again. I took a step back and whipped out the two from my side. These were smaller, but lighter and easier to maneuver.

I sliced another vampire in his ribs, but he was still able to get up. He tried again to attack, but I stabbed him again. This time I jabbed it down the side of his neck. I tried to yank it out but the others were too fast. I was knocked in the head with an elbow, and pushed to the ground. I was careful not to flare my wings. I kept them tucked. One of the vampires tried to grab my sword, but wasn't able too. Even though my wings are tipped with a thin medal, as if blades themselves, if he had cut my wing I wasn't sure if I would be able to fly back to the sanctuary. I dropped the other small one, reached for my main sword, and swung it into the next vampire. As I was pulling it out there was one behind me, I spun around slicing through his throat and I watched as his head slid from his shoulders.

With my sword back in my possession, I ran towards the last vampire. As he was jumping over my head to try to surprise me from behind, I threw my sword up in the air above me, stabbing the vampire. I looked around and saw no one else so I walked over to pull my sword out of him. I placed all three of them back, safely tucked behind my wings and at my sides. I almost forgot about the girl and was about to leave when I saw her peer through the crack between the dumpster and the wall. I was still in Angel form. I had to be. We couldn't be seen unless we took human form to try to blend in.

Right then I changed. I took a human form. I wasn't sure why. I just wanted to. I knew she saw me. I just stood there for a minute, then slowly walked towards her keeping my eyes fixed on her. She wasn't bitten. She seemed perfectly normal, other than looking terrified. I couldn't keep my eyes off of her fiery red hair and bright green eyes. She seemed average, maybe a little above average. Her white dress was dirty and her blue jacket was hanging off her shoulder. She was missing a shoe.

Angels weren't supposed to interfere this much. I wasn't quite sure what to do, but a part of me wanted to be seen. I knew what I had to do. I knelt down and reached towards her slowly without breaking my gaze into her eyes. I wanted to keep her calm. I placed my arm around her and the other on her head. I had learned this trick long ago. I can rush good feelings and put someone to sleep. It helped if someone was dying. It also helped it they needed to cover up a mess or calm someone down.

Once she was asleep I swooped her up in my arms. I tried to focus and search her mind. I couldn't exactly read minds but if they were in a deep sleep I could try to pull out small bits of information, but I wasn't very good at it. I saw the college, her dorm, and the dorm number. I turned angel again and covered her with my wings so that no one could see her being carried by me. I wanted to fly but didn't think that would be a good idea. She wasn't heavy. To me, it was like holding a feather. She seemed so frail.

"Is this what humans are like?" I thought. I studied her as I walked. I was curious about her. I wondered what it would be like to be so helpless, so scared. I found a way into her dorm but there were too rooms. I thought about laying her on the couch, but as I looked at both rooms it was like I just knew which one was hers. I placed her in her bed and covered her up. I wanted to look around a minute but knew I had to get back to the sanctuary soon.

She should be safe now, but what was I thinking? I screwed up again. I wanted to impress the others, but how would I explain this? I can't say I was just out wandering and heard her. I wasn't even supposed to be out of the sanctuary. It wasn't until after I dropped her off that I started to ask questions. Like, where was her Guardian? Why was no one else there to protect her? That's what I wanted, right? To be alone. To act alone. Something wasn't right. I need to go back to the sanctuary before they realize I was gone.

Chapter 6

ALANA

I felt groggy and confused. Like I was coming out of a surgery. It was like I couldn't remember everything. I glanced around and looked back at my best friend who now had tears running down her eyes. I looked over at the clock it was 3 AM. I think I left the party around 10 but everything seemed fuzzy. I started to get flashes of the night before.

"Well?" Lexi yelled with her voice cracking. "I thought you had gotten a ride, or maybe that you walked home. When I got here at midnight you weren't here! I went out looking for you and calling you. You left you stupid phone in my car! Hello? Alana? Answer me!"

"I'm fine." I lied. I didn't know what I was. I wasn't sure if I had just had a bad dream. I thought about telling her what I saw but all I could see was terror and worry in her eyes. What would I tell her? Would she even believe me? Before I knew it I said "I'm sorry. I was upset. I needed to cool off. I started walking home." I stopped and started staring. "I ran into someone. That's all. I would have been home sooner. Anyways it's 3 A.M, let's go to bed and we can talk tomorrow."

She gave me a look like she didn't believe me. She knows me too well. I rolled over and pretended to go to sleep. I didn't know how I would go to sleep after the night I had but somehow I still felt sleepy and I quickly drifted back to sleep.

It was Saturday and I woke up later than usual. I glanced at the clock. It was 12:30 P.M. I'm normally an early riser. I don't remember the last time I slept so much. Everything started to come back to me and I called out to Lexi. She didn't answer. She must still be sleeping. I called her name one more time before getting out of bed to look for her. I was still wearing the clothes from last night. I was still a little confused so I shuffled over to Lexi's room. She wasn't there. Although, it was hard to tell. She was the messy one. Her bed was unmade, clothes everywhere, homework all over her room, makeup and hair stuff scattered. I wondered where she was, but with her you never know. I found a note on the fridge that said going to get some food, be back soon. This was the perfect time to collect my thoughts.

Surely I should call the police. But what would I say? I pulled out my lap top to see if they reported the bodies yet and what the police thought. There was nothing. Social media was pretty quiet too, except for the usual. Had I imagined everything? Would the cops even believe me? I just want everything to go back to normal.

I heard keys in the door. I slammed my laptop shut and jumped up. Lexi came in trying to be quiet in case I was still sleeping. I tried to calm down and not act like I was scared. I threw on a big smile and said

"So what's for breakfast?"

"You're kidding right?" She said. "It's almost 2 P.M." She emphasized P.M, like I didn't already know.

The sun was shining through the windows and it seemed like a perfectly normal day.

"Is this how you feel when I sleep until noon? I waited around for you to wake up then went and got donuts."

Donuts, she really was worried for her to buy carbs. I tried to stay cheerful. I could see she was confused about last night. It wasn't like me to stay out late like that. I reached out for the chocolate covered donut and whipped it up to my mouth quickly. She tried to ask more questions, but I jokingly kept shoving donuts in my face until I finally just shoved one in hers. She laughed.

"Are we okay? I really am sorry about last night. I was worried about you. Not just because you didn't come home. I was worried about us. I promise I will make it up to you!"

"I thought that's what the donuts were!" I giggled. She gave me a smile, then she looked down. I could tell she felt shamed.

"Maybe we can do something, just us girls one night. A date. A sister date!" Lexi exclaimed with hope beaming from her eyes. That's basically what we were, sisters. Which meant we could fight and make up a million times and a million times more.

Chapter 7

LIAM

It was dark, dark enough to slip in unnoticed. Especially with the clothes I was wearing. I stayed in my human form, still cloaked. That way I could hide in the corners and shadows of the sanctuary. I found my way back to my room. After tonight I felt tired. I had a room because I needed a bed. I needed a bed because I get tired sometimes. I'm not like them, they don't get tired. They don't need rooms. They don't need anything. I don't need to sleep often. I can usually feel the rush of power and life flowing through my blood, but my flesh makes me feel weak sometimes. I need to rest. At least that would explain where I've been the past few hours. I could simply say that I was resting. I couldn't sleep though. Everything that happened kept flashing through my mind.

I had been in their territory, that's why she was alone, and that's why they weren't expecting me. I had broken the treaty. I had gotten rid of any evidence that we were there. That's normally my job anyways. The clean up crew. All I needed to do was stay under everyone's radar and listen for any information. Nobody would really miss a few street rats. At least the girl was safe. I had done something good.

The girl. What if she remembers? What if she goes to the police? I'll need to follow her. It shouldn't be too hard. I can sense her. I can sense she is sleeping now. I started to sort through the memories I saw in her mind. She's a student. It shouldn't be too hard to blend in around campus. I'll need to take a human form so I'm not recognized by others. The only problem is, what if she recognizes me? I'm not sure how it all works, but I know that the form we take is dependent on who sees us. It makes it to where we blend in. A form that is comfortable to the people around us, but doesn't stand out. If she sees me again, she might see me the same way, especially since I was half human.

The next morning I slipped out of the sanctuary again. I usually try to keep busy, so if anyone asks me questions I should be able to come up with something. I had to focus. Where was she now? I focused in on my powers. I had to locate her. I zeroed in on my senses. I had to remember everything about her for this to work. First, I heard voices but, but they weren't too loud. I smelled coffee. I tried to focus on her and only her until I appeared outside of a coffee shop near campus. It was a busy afternoon so it was pretty crowed. Which meant that it was easy to blend in. I sat in the back corner and I focused on the light near me so it would dim the corner, hiding me in the shadows.

Everyone was so busy. Too busy to notice anyone around them. The other Guardians have been around so long they have seen so many generations rise and fall, kingdoms come and go, and people changing. People don't really change though, just the things around them. Everyone seemed to have a phone in their hands focused on their social media sites. They think they are looking out seeing the world through their tiny little screens and socializing, but all I see are people staring at little boxes avoiding life around them.

It wasn't too hard to find her. She had a book and was sitting on a bench close to a window. The natural light glowed around her making her seem more alive than the people around her. She looked different then she had before. She was so focused on whatever she was reading. It looked as if she felt like she was alone. A calmness, but a determination vibrated from her. I wasn't sure if she had told anyone about the night before, but it didn't seem like it.

She looked at her watch, which was strange. I didn't think people wore watches anymore. Everyone looks at their phones. She seemed to be thinking about something, more like calculating something in her head. Time, maybe? She looked around at everyone. I was careful that she wouldn't see me. She gathered her things. It looked like a book, her phone, her keys, and her coffee which was still partially full and put them in her large bag that she hung across her chest and down at her side. She was leaving. Wherever she was going I had to follow her.

Chapter 8

ALANA

I kept thinking about the night before. The mystery man. The group of men who attacked me. Their bodies. Me waking up in my bed. It had to have been a dream. Lexi was ready for a nap. That's when she slept, during the day. She was a night owl. I always felt like I had to study quietly or clean quietly, because I did the cleaning, or I would wake the wrath of Alexis! That was not a pretty sight. Once I threw chocolate at her and walked away. I checked on her later and she had eaten the chocolate and gone to bed.

Okay. Time to study. Psychology? No not after last night. That can wait. And plus, it's taught by an intern and is pretty much a blow off class. I have already finished my Calculus homework. Class normally lets out early so I finish then. I have some reading to do for my English class or I could always study for the Bio 2 exam coming up. I figured ready would be the best way to get my mind off of everything. I loved to read. I grabbed my book bag and found the old worn out paperback used copy of the novel the Professor assigned us to read. I was already ahead of most people in the class.

Maybe I could read a few chapters and then look over my Biology notes. I plopped down on my bed. I tried to lay on my tummy and read, but that felt weird. I rolled over and held the book up. All I could think was, what if what happened last night was real. Who put me in my bed? How did they know where I lived? Would they come back? I moved over to my desk. My desk always made me focus better. Here, maybe I could concentrate. I really had nothing else to do that day. Maybe I could do my laundry. After what felt like an hour of reading, which was really only about eight minutes, I decided to do something more useful. I gathered my clothes in a laundry basket and I peeked in to see in Lexi had any clothes she needed washed, but she was sound asleep. I started to walk out my door and checked my pockets to make sure I had my phone and keys. I started to unlock the door, but ran back to my room to grab my book. Maybe I'll have better luck on the bench outside of the washroom.

I threw my keys, my phone, the book, and my change bag of quarters in the laundry basket so I could carry everything. It was nice outside. I walked in the laundry mat, started my load of clothes, and put the coins in like I always do. I grabbed my phone, keys, and book and headed down the street to a quaint coffee shop on campus. It was a nice day out so I enjoyed walking around. Most people go to the coffee shop on dates or to meet people. Sometimes people study, but that's mostly just around midterms and finals. The line wasn't long, but it seemed crowded. I ordered a Chi Late and find a cozy spot on a bench next to a window. It was my spot. Well, not really, but it was my favorite spot. I loved the lighting it gave the pages when I read. It was also slightly out of everyone's way. I'm not the type of person who likes to be in the spot light. I placed my bag next to me, put my phone and keys on my bag for easy access, because my bag is like the bag from Mary Poppins and small things get lost and enter a different universe if I leave them in there. I opened my book, found my place, and began to read.

Suddenly, I felt like someone was watching me. I kept glancing up but no one would be there. I looked down and kept reading. I usually take notes while I read, but I forgot my laptop. I felt it grow stronger. That feeling like someone was watching me. I thought the laundry must be close to being done. I looked down at my watch. The laundry only had a few minutes left so I decided to gather my things and start walking back to the laundry mat.

I arrived back at the laundry mat to switch the clothes from the washer to the dryer. I glanced up in the window and dropped the laundry basket. I thought I saw him. The guy from last night. I blinked several times because I thought I was seeing things. As soon as I saw him he disappeared. How can someone just disappear? Was I seeing things? Was stress getting to me? I sat back down. This time inside because there are cameras and I felt better knowing I was on camera. I pulled out my book and pretended to read. I still felt like I was being watched. I kept glancing up. I saw him again! I know I did. I dropped everything and ran outside. When I got past the door there was no one in sight. I really am losing my mind! I thought about chasing after the mystery man, but I wouldn't have the slightest idea where he went. I waited for my clothes to dry and went back upstairs.

On Sunday I went to church and I pretended that everything was normal. I woke Lexi up in time to go with me. She tries, but she doesn't always wake up. I spent the day cleaning our dorm and finishing homework. I made sure my clothes were ready and my alarm was set for class the next day. I made my to-do list. Lexi made fun of it, but I felt like I had to have my to-do list. My grandma encouraged me to see a psychologist after the accident. I was told that my to-do lists made me feel like I had control. I liked feeling like I had control. So much in my life has been out of my control. That's why I liked things I could control. My grades, my wardrobe (when Lexi doesn't interfere), and my to-do lists.

Monday started off pretty normal. My first class was psychology. It is a big lecture class where there are so many students that they don't even take attendance. Although, Mr. Clark, I say mister because he is some twenty-seven year old intern who gives the lecture notes and hands out the tests, is very relaxed about attendance. I walked in fifteen minutes early as usual. I rushed to my spot that I try to sit in every class. It's not assigned to me, I just like routine and I think it has the best view of the board. Mr. Clark stammered in late, as usual. He says it's to give students extra time, because the time structure is too strict. If you ask me, he just wants everyone to like him so he can be the cool teacher. Which he is. Lexi even heard rumor of his good looks and sat in on a lecture one day. She learned nothing of course.

I started to get my notebook and pen out when I saw him! It was the man with the curly blond hair. I froze. I didn't know what to do. I glanced around and looked back and he was still there. He was staring at me. The same way he stared at me Friday night. He was in the back like he had just walked in and grabbed a seat. No one really seemed to notice him. I had been in this class several times and never seen him before. He looked about my age, maybe a little older. So I guess it's possible he's a student here. So I hadn't imagined it. Did he kill those guys? What did he do with the bodies? How did he know where my dorm was and how to get in? How did he know which bed was mine? Is he following me? What if this was some sick joke to scare some college girl. Mr. Clark started the lecture. I tried to focus on him. I tried to take notes, but I kept glancing at the mystery guy. Who is he? I knew that after class I would run up and confront him. As soon as Mr. Clark dismissed class I gathered my things, threw them in my back pack, and ran towards him. He wasn't there. I couldn't find him anywhere. How did I miss him? The bigger question I asked myself was, will I see him again?

Chapter 9

LIAM

I knew she saw me at the laundry mat. I tried to disappear. I should have known she would see me, I should have been more careful. I tried to avoid being in angel form, and I tried to avoid her Guardian by staying in human form. Not that they wouldn't have noticed what I was, but it wouldn't have been very obvious in a crowd. When she saw me I had to turn. I didn't see her Guardian nearby. I saw her chase after me. If she didn't tell anyone about the night before, she would now. I hadn't even thought about how it might feel to see me again. If I looked the same again it might frighten her. I didn't think about that until I saw the look on her face. She seemed terrified, but also curious. She seemed confused. I wasn't sure how humans could feel so many things at once. A part of me felt like I needed to be more careful, or just give up and let her be. A part of me liked being seen.

I didn't follow her everywhere. I knew her Guardian would sense something in her, her fear and confusion, and stay closer to her. I still felt nervous about her being followed by the Fallen. So far she was safe, but I began only checking on her in public places. It was easy to check on her on campus. With so many people walking around in so many different directions. All in a hurry, each of them going to a specific place. Most likely following the same paths they take every day. I've noticed how people like to feel comfortable and don't like change. If you sit back and watch they seem to do the same things over and over. They look like ants in a colony. It wouldn't be too hard to blend in. Basically I just needed to look busy. I tried to scan the crowd and see if anyone stood out, if anyone else was watching her.

I saw her slip into a class. There were so many people I felt confident that I wouldn't look too suspicious. Again, she saw me. I could tell she recognized me because she kept looking back at me. It would look to suspicious to walk out, and I obviously could not disappear in plain sight. I didn't hear a single word of the lecture, I kept looking around to see if anyone one seemed to be watching her. I'm sure her Guardian was close. I could tell she was trying to focus on the lecture but she didn't seem to be taking many notes, and she kept looking back at me.

At first it was amusing. She would pretend not to see me, or she would pretend to look at the clock or look at other people. Once she dropped her pen and glanced at me when she bent down to get it. I didn't mean to but I gave her a small smirk. After that she seemed to glance back every few seconds and give me a stare like she was asking me a million questions with her eyes. I could tell the lecture was coming to an end and as soon as people started to get up, I slipped out.

After I made it out I changed back into my angel form. I started to feel pretty confident that she was safe and that everything would work out until I felt something. I could sense someone who wasn't supposed to be here. I sensed danger. I searched until I saw him. He was looking at the girl. I recognized him from the fight the other night. One of the vampires must have gotten away. How did I let that happen? I thought

I had cleaned everything up, that I left nothing. How could I be so stupid, so careless? He wasn't the only one here. I could sense it. I had to leave or they would recognize me. I had to come up with a plan. I needed to get her to safety. But what would I do? I couldn't just tell her Guardian that she is in danger without giving away what I had done and I couldn't just keep following her. They would notice my absence. I had to do something and I had to do it now.

She was walking alone. I knew her Guardian would catch up soon. No doubt he would be distracted by the others nearby. I had to get her alone. She had her book bag strapped on to one shoulder and wasn't zipped all the way. If I can just make the wind blow just enough I can get her bag to blow off of her shoulder and spill out behind the wall of the building. I was pretty good with manipulating wind. Luckily she wasn't very graceful. Just as I planned, it fell off and was open just enough to scatter some papers and highlighters. I tried not to laugh as she scampered around collecting her things. For a moment I thought how fun it would be to stay out of sight and play pranks on people. I felt foolish, distracted. I blinked towards her and put her to sleep. I picked her up and shielded her with my wings. I was careful to grab her bag so that I didn't leave anything behind. I had to find somewhere to keep her. The only place I could think of was the sanctuary. I have to sneak her in.

You can't just blink into the sanctuary, there are rules against that. The closest thing I could do is blink nearby and maybe fly her to my window. If not, I'd have to carry her in the front door. Humans are forbidden in the sanctuary. That's pretty much a number one rule, but I couldn't just take her back to her dorm. I couldn't trust that her guardian would be there when they need to be. This was my doing. I had to fix it. For her to be safe I need to get rid of all the threats. I blinked as close to the sanctuary as possible. My window was still open so I could fly right in without anyone noticing me. I carried her in but didn't know where to put her. I placed her on my bed because it seemed like a better idea than dumping her on the floor. Her hair fell in her face as I laid her down. I always thought it was interesting how imperfect humans are. I looked her over, other than her red hair she seemed very ordinary. Clumsy sometimes, even. I wondered what it would be like it we weren't around to step in. It bothered me, not being able to see her face. I don't know why. Without hesitation, I gently wiped her hair out of her face.

I heard the door rush open. Before I could even think I saw Atticus there staring at the girl on the bed.

"What have you done?" He said in a hushed but firm voice.

It didn't even occur to me how this may look. Grabbing a human, sneaking her in, and putting her on my bed. Not only that I was sitting there on the bed looking at her. I didn't know how to explain that I was just trying to keep her safe.

"It's not like that. She's in trouble." I pleaded.

"You mean you're in trouble. What did you think you were doing?" He seemed concerned. Not only for her, but for me. He looked at her like he had known her. Like he cared for her, specifically for her. How could I be so stupid? "Did you think I wouldn't notice you following her? And now you bring her here." He scolded. She's his mission.

I tried to explain everything, but before I realized it I was yelling. Someone must have heard me because I felt a presence blink it. Great, it was Baron. I couldn't read his expression. It looked like confusion, but mostly he seemed pleased. Probably pleased that I had once again proved that I'm not worthy. I could tell he was trying not to smile. He blinked away before I could stop him, then Baron reappeared. This time with Idris. She was easy to read, shock was written on her face. She glanced at Baron, me, the girl, and Atticus, then back at me.

"Explain yourself." Her voice sounded like thunder. I have never really feared her before now.

Once I explained everything Baron stepped right in to suggest banishment. The permanent kind. I'm sure in his mind he could already see me being stripped of my wings, as easy to him as a quick snip. Atticus has always tried to protect me, even now it took everything in him not to fight Baron. He would never do that though. He just stood there in attention. It was quiet. Too quiet.

"Surely there is something we can do. He was trying to protect her. He's still learning our way." Atticus said.

"You're right. But, he still broke the rules. For this he must be banished. We will not strip him of his wings, but until he learns to obey he is not allowed back at the sanctuary. No one is to speak of this to anyone. Is that clear?" They both nodded.

She looked at me. "You need to leave." She said.

"What about the girl?" I asked.

"She is Atticus' mission, not yours." She scolded.

I don't know what came over me but I rushed to the girl and blinked her out. I didn't know where I was going until we got there. I must have been thinking about this place when I blinked.

Chapter 10

ALANA

I felt confused. I didn't really know where I was. I had that same cloudy dream like daze that I felt the morning after I woke up after the attack. Everything was kind of blurry. I tried to blink a few times, but it was dark and my eyes hadn't adjusted yet. I wasn't in my room. Immediately I felt my whole body illuminate fear. My mind was racing and I immediately thought of the man who kept following me. I wasn't sure if he was nearby. All I knew is that I had to get out. My hands were tied and I was laying on a hard floor. It felt hot and humid, but had a slight chill. It was like I was outside, but I definitely felt like in was inside somewhere. There wasn't any air-conditioning. It smelled like I was outside, but I got the feeling I was in a house. There was a window open and there was a little light shining in. It wasn't quite a full moon, but it was bright enough that when my eyes adjusted I could start to make out shapes and objects.

I was in a room. It looked kind of like a bedroom, but it was larger than some people's houses. I don't know what had happened here, but something wasn't right. It looked old. There were cracks in the walls, dust and spider webs everywhere, and most of the furniture was broken or leaning. There didn't seem to be anyone around me so I thought it would be the perfect time to escape. I didn't see my purse or phone anywhere.

I looked down. I was still wearing my cream colored loose shirt, high wasted floral print skirt and a pair of white sandals. Why had I dressed so girly today? It would be hard to get far in this. I needed jeans and tennis shoes. Either way, I would make do. I wasn't going anywhere with my hands still tied. I saw some broken glass by the French doors leading to a balcony. I could use it to cut the rope and run through the door and keep it as a weapon if I need to. Maybe it would be better to climb down the balcony? There's no telling what would be behind that door, and I'm not sure I want to find out.

Before I could reach the glass I felt someone else come into the room. It was weird. I didn't hear the door open. Maybe there was another door I hadn't seen. Or maybe I was so focused on getting my hands free that I hadn't noticed them come in. I stayed still and quiet. I don't know why. It's not like I was kidnaped by a bear. It was him. I knew it was him I couldn't see him, but I could tell it was him. He was standing in the corner of the room where a shadow hid his face. He didn't move and didn't say anything.

Finally he said, "I wouldn't do that if I were you."

I didn't know if he knew I was trying to escape, or yell, or if he saw me trying to get to the broken glass.

Now what? I had never heard his voice, but I saw him step out into the light so I could see him.

"There's no need to scream, no one will hear you." He said.

"What are you going to do with me? Let me go." I insisted. Really? That's what I had to say? I couldn't think of anything more clever? It didn't matter. He seemed to smirk again. Not in a threatening way. It almost seemed like he was annoyed. How was he annoyed? He was the one that took me! What was his deal and why had he taken me? Where were we? It was then that I realized I didn't even know how long I had been out. I could be anywhere. I had to find out where we were and why he took me.

I tried to calm myself.

"I'm Alana." I said. He didn't say anything. "And you are?" I asked.

He just stared at me and paced back and forth. He seemed nervous. Maybe if I could get him talking I could figure out how to get out of here.

"Is this your house?" I asked. He was quiet for a second, then replied no. "So, what are we doing here?" I asked, hoping I could get him talking. Nothing. He just kept slowing pacing, then leaned against a wall. "I guess we're not here to talk." I said sarcastically under my breath. "Listen, I won't tell anyone what you did. I haven't told anyone yet, and if I haven't told anyone about the other night I won't tell them about this. Just please, let me go home." Still nothing. "I have school I need to get back to and my roommate will miss me. We're best friends. And I have a lot of homework I need to do. I don't have time to… To… What am I even doing here? What are you doing with me?"

"I'm keeping you safe!" He finally yelled and slammed his fist into the wall.

What did he mean? Keeping me safe? Safe from who? Was he crazy? Was he protecting me from the guys the other night? Didn't he get rid of them? Who were they anyways? What have I gotten myself into? Whatever is going on I need to get home.

"Okay, fine. I can play this game. Just untie me and tell me what's going on." I pleaded. "You wouldn't understand." he mumbled.

"Try me." I said. He looked over at me then walked over. I flinched because I didn't know what he was about to do. He stood behind me, knelt down and gently untied the knots. He didn't cut them. He took his time and untied them. Something felt weird about him being so close. I thought it would be foolish to run when he was done. Obviously he could outrun and outfight me. If I was getting out of here I would have to slip out. "I need answers." I demanded.

"You need to stay here." He said quietly.

Somehow I had fallen asleep. I don't remember falling asleep. I'm not sure how he keeps doing that. I was still untied. I didn't see him anywhere and the sun was starting to come up. I quietly walked across the room. I grabbed the doorknob and turned it. The whole house seemed like an old plantation house from an old war. It was huge. It almost seemed like a castle. It must have been abandoned because there were cracks, overgrown plants, and grass and ivy everywhere. It felt like a fairytale. Not the being kidnapped part, but the house. I got the feeling deep in my gut that something bad had happened here.

The stairs looked like something out of a bridal magazine, except that maybe a tornado had gone through them. Through the whole house really. The stairs were barely there. I was afraid that they would give out with me walking on them. How had he gotten me up here? Maybe I would be safer climbing down the balcony. I went back to the room that he had kept me in and made my way towards the balcony. There were vines and ivy everywhere. It seemed strong enough to hold me, but I don't really know anything about climbing. I was only two stories up and it was grass, old gardens, and statues everywhere. There was nothing and no one around, except a big stone and metal gate around the property which seemed to extend as far as I could see.

I grabbed the vines and started climbing down. It was harder than it looked. My hands hurt and I had never realized how heavy I actually was. There were bits or glass and thorns scratching my arms and legs on the way down. A few times I lost my footing, but it didn't take long for me to get down. Well, mostly I fell down. When I was a few feet from the ground I slipped and hit stone. It hurt, but I was alright. Just a few cuts and bruises. Mostly on my behind.

"Having trouble?" I heard.

"Have you been standing there the whole time?" I yelled.

"Pretty much."

I looked around to see if there was anywhere I could run or anything I could grab to defend myself with, but I knew that would be a waste of effort. He started to walk away slowly, but looked back as if to ask if I was coming too. I followed.

We were walking towards a garden. It was very overgrown and had a lot of stone statues, bird baths, and some overgrown walkways. It was so overgrown that I couldn't see where I was going. It reminded me of home. Well, my grandparents' home. They had a large garden too, and a pond. But it wasn't this overgrown. This house looked like it hadn't been touched in decades.

"There are… people after you." He said. He seemed to have to choose his words carefully.

"Who?" I asked. "And why are you helping me?"

"I… Protect people." He said. Again, very slow like he was trying to explain without telling me too much. We kept walking. "They were going to kill you. I saved you." He said.

"How do you know? And you still haven't told me who they are."

"Like I said, you wouldn't believe me."

"Like I said… Try me."

"You just need to stay here until you are safe again, then I'll leave you alone." He stopped and was staring at a flower. He reached up and touched it gently. He looked sad. He turned around and looked at me. "It's going to rain. You need to get back inside." He said.

"How? Do you want me to climb the window again?" I snipped. I saw that's annoying smirk again.

"If that's what you prefer." Instead he led me up the stairs. He just showed me where to step.

"I still don't know your name." I said.

In one word he replied, "Liam", and shut the door.

I stayed really quiet and listened by the door. I never saw him leave, but I don't think he was guarding the door. Maybe he went to sleep. This was the perfect opportunity. I started to look around some more to see if there was another way. There was only one I could see. I climbed down the vines again. This time I did a little better. I wasn't quite an expert, but I survived. I made my way down the road to the gate as fast as I could. The gate wasn't even closed. It was a black metal gate that was old and broken, but slightly wedged open. Just enough for me to slip out.

It was mostly woods but I thought I heard cars. I found the road and recognized where we were. Surprisingly enough we were about ten minutes from town, so I started walking. I wasn't entirely sure I was going the right way. It's a small town so it was hard to tell, but I would find out eventually. It seemed like I walked forever before someone pulled over and asked if I needed help. I still wasn't sure what to tell anyone. Surely I should go to the police. Any sane person would. Honestly, I just wanted to get home. I had no idea how to explain any of this, and somchow I felt like I trust him. Liam.

Something about the man driving the car that seemed familiar. He was tall and stiff. He couldn't have been but a few years older than me. It looked like he might have been in the military or something. Even though he looked big and tough, there was something soft about him. For some reason he almost reminded me of my dad. Not that they looked alike, just he seemed fatherly. Maybe protective is the word I was looking for. I was nervous to get in the car, but it sure beet walking. I told him that I was riding a bike around town and when it rained my bike slipped off the road and broke. I told him I had been walking back for a while and couldn't find my phone to call for help. He looked suspicious but didn't say anything. I almost got the feeling he knew something was up. I told him I was a college student and needed a ride to campus. I said I didn't want to worry about my bike, it was broken anyways. I'm not sure if he bought my story, especially with what I was wearing but he didn't seem to want to pry.

Chapter 11

LIAM

When I blinked us out I wasn't sure where I was taking her. I usually like to fly. I like feeling the freedom and control it gives me, but I didn't have time for that now. Atticus could outfly me or follow me. Maybe that's what made me think of this place. I've only been here once, and swore that I would never come back again. It looked just as it had before. It pained me to be here, but it's the only place that no one would look. She might think to look here, but at least it will by me some time to come up with a plan. It was night by now. I carried the girl up the stairs to the farthest room. It was the largest room in the house. Well, the largest bedroom. There was no way out of it except through the door or through the window and as far as I knew she couldn't fly. I saw the bed, but I didn't want to lay her there. Instead, I found a small old style couch near the window. It was a dusty blue velvet with some tears and stains, but it was the best I could do for now.

I knew she had a little more time before she would wake up. I wanted to get out of that room. I shut the door and paced around the house. A part of me was curious about it. I wanted to explore it to know all of its history, but most of me wanted to fly as far away as I could. Idris brought me here when I was younger. I always knew I was different. I kept asking Idris about who I was and why I was different. That's when she took me here. She explained everything. She explained how my father fell in love with a human and I was conceived. She told me how he lost his wings and fled here. She told me that because of him my mother was killed. I barely survived, but he left me. He left her and he left me. I don't know why she took me in. Maybe it was to keep an eye on me. This is where my mother was kept. This is where I was born. This is where she was slaughtered.

I couldn't help but feel anger stirring inside me boiling to the top of my being. The other guardians could control themselves better than I could. Maybe it was because they have been around so much longer, or maybe it was because I was different. That's why Idris was so mad. I wasn't like him. I hadn't fallen for this girl. I just wanted to make everything right. I'm not like him. I'm nothing like him. Still the thought of him taking Catharine here, and me taking this girl here made me hate myself even more. I'm not going to leave her like he left Catherine.

I could sense her starting to wake up. I blinked in to check on her but stayed in the corner where it was dark. I should have walked in through the door. She wouldn't have been used to people suddenly appearing. I could tell she was terrified. She seemed like she was trying to remain calm. As much as she talked, I tried to stay as quiet as possible. I didn't want to give away too much. I'm sure I have already said and done more that I should. I left her there. At least maybe she could get some rest.

I wanted to get outside. Everything about that house made me feel miserable. I have never been sick before, but I imagine it's close to this.

The sun had already come up. There were dew drops glistening and reflecting the light in every direction. I could see beauty of the morning. In every drop was a rainbow. A promise to humanity. Rainbows are supposed to signify protection. I let my wings stretch out and soak up the sun and mist. That's when I heard her.

I knew she couldn't see me. I thought maybe I should say something to stop her from trying to climb down the side of the house, but I didn't. I had to admit, she was stubborn. She had a fire about her. Her red hair reflected the light of the Sun, giving it glow that looked like fire. Her clumsiness was amusing. It took her a long time to finally get the bottom before she fell. I tried my hardest not to laugh. She looked up and saw me and shock fell on her face. I could tell I was going to have a hard time keeping her in line. I signaled for her to follow me to the garden. She kept asking questions and I tried to answer as coy as possible.

I was distracted though. There was something about the garden. It was as if I could picture my mom here. I never really knew what she looked like. I never dared to ask, even though I know Idris had seen her before. Something about the graceful bloom of the flowers sent my mind reeling with my own questions that I fought to ignore. I could sense the rain in the air. Honestly I didn't mind if she got drenched in rain. I could care less, but I figured it would be best if she was back inside. If they were looking for us I didn't want it to be as easy as her standing on the front yard. She joked about having to climb back up the wall, which I would have loved to see her try.

Instead I helped her up the stairs. I couldn't fly or blink her up without questions so I had her follow my footsteps up the stairs so she wouldn't fall through. She started to lose her footing one time and started to grab me. She barely brushed my arm. I know she didn't want help from me, and I don't even think she knew she touched me. It felt strange to me, for someone to touch me. I've touched humans before, but I have never been in human form so long, long enough for anyone to reach out to me and surprise me. I decided to leave her alone. I had to see if anyone was close to us.

Chapter 12

ALANA

I made it back to my dorm. The stranger didn't say much, but he seemed kind and concerned. Honestly I seemed kind of distracted by how attractive he was. Something about him reminded me of Liam. Liam had this perfectness about him. Maybe it was the way he held himself. Kind of a self-righteousness. Even though he couldn't be much more than six feet tall, he seemed to stand as though he was ten feet tall. The way he walked was like an Olympic swimmer gliding through the water on their way to gold. I pulled out my phone ready to call the police. Even though he didn't harm me, kidnapping is a crime. That, and I need to know what happened the other night. I tired collecting my thoughts. I had no clue what I would tell the police or where to start. How would I not sound like a drunk college student, or some crazy person with another abduction story? It sure sounds like Aliens when I try to talk about it.

As I was considering what I would say, Lexi walked in.

"Alana! What is going on? I've been calling you where have you been all weekend? I thought maybe you went home without me."

I wasn't sure where to start do I start with my crazy night in an abandoned mansion, or do I tell her about the night of the party where I got attacked by men who were then attacked by an invisible guy who keeps popping up everywhere? As I gathered my thoughts, trying to organize them and rationalize them there was a knock at the door. Since I wasn't doing much talking Lexi seemed to ignore me and go straight for the door.

It was Liam! I was speechless. What do I do now? Would he take her too? It still seemed weird because I still felt like he really didn't want to harm me. Something about him seemed different. Fake is more like it. He had a gorgeous grin on his face he was wearing a different outfit. He was wearing a white collared shirt that looked like a school golf shirt. He seemed preppy, like maybe he should drive a Lamborghini. This boy who was standing in front of my friend seemed less mysterious and less intense. His curly blond hair fell by his warm green eyes, and there was a small dimple that seemed to kiss his cheek. How did I miss that before? Oh yeah, maybe because he didn't smile long enough for me to see it.

"Sorry to bother you but Laney forgot her backpack on our study date. I know she can't live without it so I thought I would return it. I'm Liam" He said all charming.

Lexi's eyes light up and so did her smile. She turned to me gleaming. I could have killed him for calling me Laney! That's it. If I couldn't kill him, I'd at least get one good punch in, right in his dimple!

"So this is why your phone hasn't been working?" She accused me.

"Uhh.. I'm sorry Lexi, can I talk to Alana alone?" Liam said.

She gave me a look and grabbed her keys and said it was okay because she was just leaving anyways, even though she had just gotten back. I was silently pleading with her to stay but off she went.

"Listen, I'm sorry. I shouldn't have just taken you like that. I'm sure you were scared." I'm sure he wasn't done talking but I interrupted him anyways.

"Scared? Are you kidding me? After God knows what happened the other night, then you kidnap me. Now you follow me to my dorm and act like everything is okay! I should have you arrested." I declared.

"No please, let me try to explain. The guys I fought the other night are.... Bad guys. They are mad that I fought them. That's what I do. I protect people from them. Now they are targeting you because you got away. I was only trying to protect you. They have been following you and know where your dorm is. The moment you are alone they will attack you."

I didn't know what to think. He seemed so sincere.

"You can think of me as an undercover cop, or a body guard. I know this is hard to understand. It's just that you need to be watched until I can take care of these guys. They could be anywhere." He said.

"Well then I will call the cops and they can give me a restraining order."

"A restraining order won't work and the cops can't help. Please trust me." As he said those words 'trust me' I felt a warmness rush over me. It was as if I trusted him with my life. I didn't know what was going on. At the front of my mind was that I trusted him.

He left and Lexi came back into the room with an amused look on her face. "So! Who is he? Tell me everything!" She begged.

"There is nothing to tell. He is in one my classes." Which wasn't completely a lie. He had gone to one of my lectures.

"Seriously Laney, you don't tell me anything anymore. We never do anything together anymore."

"Lex.... It's just that I've been busy I'm sorry."

"You're still mad about the party aren't you?"

"No, no. It's not that."

"Then what? How can I make it up to you? Ooooh! I have an idea! A date! A girls date, just the two of us! I'll even pay. And I'll buy the popcorn! But no kissing on the first date. Oh who am I kidding, there might be kissing." She snickered.

"Oh gosh. Umm… Throw in a coke and skittles and leave out the kissing and it's a date." I said. She seemed to feel better after that. Honestly, All I could think about was showering, getting some good sleep, and catching up on my homework.

The next week I tried to act normal. Liam showed up with coffee at 7 am to walk me to my classes. At least I'm getting free coffee out of this little arrangement. He said he couldn't always be around, that there was someone else protecting me when he was gone. It made me feel nervous, but also made me open my eyes and become more perceptive about the people around me. Before I was always so focused on getting to class, or staring at my phone. It made me feel uncomfortable to look at people. Now I found myself constantly studying others around me.

When no one was around Liam seemed to fade back to the mysterious man I first met. I couldn't quite figure him out. Something was different about him. The week continued. He mostly left me alone, and when we were together he didn't say much. I don't know if it was something I did. I tried not to think about it, but he was hard to ignore.

I started getting ready for my date with Lexi that night. I wasn't going to let anything ruin it. No boys, no school, just us having fun. It was starting to get chillier outside, at least at night time, so I threw on some leggings a long loose top (which was almost a dress on me because I'm 5'2). I decided I wanted to enjoy tonight so I curled my long hair and threw on some accessories. I even did my makeup more than I usually do. Lexi came up behind me and sprayed me with her perfume. I thought I was going to choke to death. We took her car again, it seems like we always took her car. She would never say she was embarrassed by my hand-me-down Honda, but she certainly prefers her Lexus.

We pulled up and got in line for tickets. I started to grab my wallet, but she reminded me that she was a gentlemen and was paying for me. I laughed so hard I snorted and turned around to make sure no one heard me. He was standing right there. Liam. He ran his hand through his hair and said hi. It was weird. I've never seen him run his hand through his hair. He always seemed so stiff, so perfect. But there he was, standing right behind me.

Chapter 13

LIAM

I should have known she would try to escape again. I guess I assumed she wouldn't try the same thing twice especially in the rain. I've got to admit. She's got spunk. But spunk isn't going to keep her alive. I grabbed her bag and headed to her house. I wanted to gain her trust. The only way I knew how was to influence her. As Guardians, we can't make people do anything. It would be against their free will. But, we can influence them. Maybe not quite in choices as much as in feelings. Like when someone is in a car wreck, we can calm them and help them focus to miss another vehicle. Sometimes if someone is angry and going to hurt someone, we can try to calm them. I influenced her to trust me. I think it worked she seemed to relax a little in my presence.

Atticus wasn't allowed to see me and I knew how he was about the rules. I kept my distance. I know he kept a closer eye on Alana, but it was like he was going out of his way to avoid me. While he was watching Alana I was hunting. I felt myself getting more and more tired. I also felt like I would start to get hungry or hot. I guess I had been staying in human form more than I ever have. Being in human form was good for us because it showed us a lot about humans. We could relate to hunger, or cold, or anger better if we experienced it. We were among some of the only type of angels able to do so. It was also a curse because of the temptations that came with staying in flesh. I tried to stay in form as little as possible.

I knew she had planned a date with her roommate tonight. I couldn't let her be out by herself even if she was with a friend. I knew Atticus would probably be nearby, but I didn't want to rely on him alone. Although, if I had to rely on a guardian it would be him. For a moment I felt nervous about what to wear. I told myself it was because I needed to fit in. I didn't have a whole lot of clothes. We didn't need much. I mean we don't just run around in angel gowns all the time. We wear clothes. We can wear pretty much whatever we like, especially while on mission. Around the sanctuary we try to stay with plainer clothes. That's what I had mostly. Dark worn blue jeans and black or white shirts. I found an old green collard polo shirt that looked like something a college boy would wear.

Instinctively I wanted to blink to where she was, but I knew better. I had to act human. I didn't have a car like some Guardians did, so I walked. I started looking for her until I heard her laugh. I had never heard her laugh in that way before. She seemed so happy. I walked up behind her just as she turned around. I guess I expected her to be shocked, instead she seemed annoyed. I tried to play it cool.

"Hey Lexi, Alana. What are you doing here?" I said trying to keep a smile on my face. I noticed that Alana looked different. Most days she wore very little makeup and she liked to wear her hair back, especially on school days. Tonight she looked different.

"Oh my gosh! Liam! Fancy meeting you here." She giggled annoyingly.

"Yeah, thought I'd get out and see a movie. What are you two planning on seeing?" I asked.

Before Alana could even get a word in Lexi replied, "Oh you know, the latest Rom Com!" I gave a confused look.

"Romantic comedy." Alana interrupted.

Lexi cut in "Well I wanted to see the new Fifty Shades movie!"

"Actually, we're here to see the Beauty and the Beast remake" Alana said shyly as if she was embarrassed.

"Is it any good?" I asked, and then felt stupid realizing that they hadn't seen it yet.

"Umm... It's Beauty and the Beast. Laney has only waited her whole life to see it on the big screen. And it's got Emma Watson! So it's basically the non-cartoon version of Beauty and the Beast." Lexi chimed in.

I stood there looking a little confused.

"You have seen beauty and the Beast right? Everyone has. It's a Disney classic! You should watch it with us!" Lexi said.

"I would love to if you wouldn't mind." I said watching the disbelief in Alana's face.

"Why don't you two go find seats and I'll get our food." Lexi said.

I was lost. I had never been to a movie before. Alana seemed to be studying me. I was taking everything in. The people all around me, the smells one particular smell. Alana. She smelled different than usual. I almost forgot to look for any Fallen, or to even look out for Atticus which I had realized wasn't even there until I noticed another presence. This one was different. It was hard to place. It wasn't a threatening presence, but it wasn't an Angel.

Someone approached Lexi and I thought she was going to scream. She jumped up and hugged the mysterious man. I could tell he was the one I was sensing. As soon as he got close enough to me I could tell he knew who I was, or at least what I was. He stared me down and seemed to be trying to protect Lexi. Guardians don't take human form unless their mission is in danger, so maybe he thought Lexi was in danger. Just then, it occurred to me. What if to him he just sensed an Angel? What if he didn't know if I was a Guardian or a Fallen? Lexi invited him along too, which I could sense made Alana mad.

"Why don't you girls find spots and we can carry the drinks and food?" I suggested.

"Perfect!" Lexi exclaimed.

I saw Alana scowl at her friend in a joking way which I didn't quite understand. My thought was interrupted when I turned to the guy.

"What are you? And what are you doing with Lexi?" He demanded.

Now that he was closer I knew what he was. He was one of the last werewolves. Most were extinct or in hiding, but some still roamed around. Werewolves weren't like angels. They were once people. During the great wars and famine in the earlier days of creation men begged the Father to give them strength and power like a Guardian to watch over their people. When the Father refused they went behind his back to the first of The Fallen. Just as Lucifer promised eternal life to the Vampires, he promised power to the tribe of people.

First they must sacrifice an animal. They received power, but with that power came a great curse. They were gifted power stronger than any man on Earth but only during a full moon. With that power also came a blood lust. Instead of protecting their people, many of the wolf men slaughtered their people. Through the years they have been hunted, but some remain. He was one of them.

"I'm Liam. I'm a Guardian. I'm here to protect Alana." I said firmly. I'm not sure if he was here to hurt Alana or not. I didn't sense him as a danger and he seemed more interested in Lexi than Alana. "What are you doing here?" I demanded.

"First, if you are a Guardian than why are you hanging out with her? Second, I'm Caleb Channing. I was here to see a movie, until I ran into you." He scolded. "Listen, I don't know what your deal is. I'm here and I'm going to make sure you don't hurt Lexi or her friend."

"I'm not going to let either of them get hurt." I glared back at him.

He brushed my shoulder as he walked passed me with the drinks. I grabbed the popcorn and followed.

I sat next to Alana, which I could sense made her feel a little uncomfortable. I tried not to get too close to her, but I didn't want Lexi to be suspicious, although she seemed completely focused on the wolf, Caleb Channing. Alana kept glancing up at me like she was studying every move I made. I tried not to stand out. I tried to slouch a little, which was very uncomfortable for me. I kept my arms on my lap, then tried to cross them, then I stretched them out across the seat around Alana, which felt weird and after the weird look from Alana and the threatening look from the wolf I folded my arms in my lap again. I wasn't trying to make some move on her. I just didn't know what to do with my arms. I think she could tell I was uncomfortable I saw her raise an eyebrow and her lips just slightly curled into a smile.

I guess it was amusing watching me squirm around in the seat. The whole thing was strange for me. I had a hard time following the movie and I didn't like to sit for so long. Movies seemed like a waste of time to me, but everyone else seemed to be enjoying it. There was a moment where her hand brushed mine. I could tell it was an accident, she looked horrified. She crossed her arms as well, so we both ended up watching the movies with our arms crossed. Lexi and wolf-boy on the other hand were all cuddled up. He kept glaring at me though. What made me even madder was the way he kept looking at Alana.

When the movie was over Lexi said that Caleb invited everyone over to his place. No doubt it was to keep an eye on me. Alana declined and I was relieved. I offered to walk Alana home. I saw Lexi sigh from happiness. She thought her friend was going on some romantic stroll, but Caleb leaned over and said, "If anything happens to her I will hunt you down." I didn't take it as too much of a threat. Yes, a wolf can do some damage on angels, but I've got the upper hand by far.

I tilted my head and signaled Alana to follow. At first it was silent. Neither of us said anything. Then she asked, "You have never seen Beauty and the Beast?"

I smiled and shook my head, trying to play it cool.

"Have you ever been to a movie?" She asked curiously.

"No." I replied. She was just quiet, like she was sorting through a million more questions in her head.

"Where are you from?" She asked.

"Here." I replied. She narrowed her eyes at me. We stopped under a street light and she seemed in shock, like she saw something. I knew she couldn't have. "Are you alright?" I asked.

"Something about you." She replied. I was so focused on her and her questions I hadn't noticed that we were being followed. Someone came up behind me and tried to stab me. I sensed the danger early enough to push her out of the way and spin around. I opened my razor sharp wings and transformed. An angels wings are shapeless and colorless. They can appear as shimmering gold, rain, snow, or hard metal. They took the form of whatever they needed to be including a shield and that's what I needed right now. There were only three of them. I was quick to get in front of Alana and throw her towards a wall so they couldn't get to her. This time they weren't vampires, they were Fallen. Which meant they had all the strength and skills as I did.

I stabbed the first guy and pulled him close to use as a shield since my wings were protecting Alana. I drove my sword into the second guy and dropped the guy I was holding to grab my second sword. He put up more of a fight, but I stabbed him near the heart. He wasn't quiet dead. He was able to blink himself and the other two bodies away.

Suddenly I felt week. A sharp pain ripped through my side and I fell over. Alana rushed towards me. I came to and realized she was crying. I looked down and saw that I was stabbed in my side by my ribs. It wasn't very deep. To me it was like a scratch. My arm was also dripping blood. The sanctuary is where we get healed and I couldn't go there. For now I would have to patch myself up. But first, I had to figure out what to tell Alana. During most of the fighting I was in Angel form. She wouldn't have seem any of the fight, just me disappearing and reappearing in front of her with blood all over me and some weird force pushing her into a wall. "I'm fine." I tried to reassure her.

"You're not fine you're bleeding." She insisted.

"I know you didn't see anything but…" Before I could finish she interrupted.

"I saw….." She stopped. "I don't know what I saw." She said. She couldn't have seen anything. I was in Angel form. I had to get her back to her dorm where Atticus would be before they came back. The only way I thought to do that was to blink her back. Lexi still wasn't home. I was thankful for that. I needed to rest for a minute. I sat down on her couch. She looked so stunned she might pass out. I was worried she might hit her head but it hurt too much to get up. She just stood there for a while staring at me.

"I can stitch it up if I have to. I can sew. Kind of, my grandmother taught me." She said. She can sew? That's what she has to say? Not who am I? What am I? Get out. You need a doctor. 'I can sew'.

Chapter 14

ALANA

"I can sew." I felt so stupid. I think I was in shock. I'm not sure what happened that night. I'm not sure what I saw. I kept flashing back to moments earlier. I knew there was something different about him. Then it was like I was being pushed away. Liam just disappeared before my eye. I just stood there. I didn't know what to do. Then I was pushed again against a building. I almost couldn't breathe. Then, I saw a shimmering gold. Something was reflecting the light from the lamp post it seemed to blind me, but there was nothing there. I kept seeing flashes of dark shadows flying around. One second I could see them, the next second nothing was there I was alone. Then I was like I was looking at silver blinds. But not like they were in front of me. It was like they were transparent. Like one of the transparency machines they used to use in school. Like someone drew sliver blinds on one of the clear pages and projected it onto a screen, but the screen was real life. Mostly I saw nothing. It was just the glimpses. I thought I could see Liam's outline, but it was like mist, like rain or snow maybe. But it wasn't him, what I saw was nearly ten feet tall.

After a few minutes Liam appeared back in front of me like a flash. He was covered in blood. First I noticed a large cut on his arm several inches long, but not very deep. Then I saw him grabbing his side. There was blood oozing out. He was laying on the concrete. I hovered over him in disbelief. In a split second we went from the ally to my dorm room. How did he do that? I know it was him. Now I was standing in the kitchenette and he hobbled over to our small couch. That's when I told him I could sew him up. He looked confused, which astounded me, because I was the one who should be confused.

"I'll be fine." He assured me. "I need to go somewhere, but I'll be back. You should be okay for now." And just like that he disappeared. There was blood on the couch. I started to clean it up. I know tricks for getting different stains out. After everything was clean I started to clean myself up. I was worried about Liam, but how would I know if he was okay. Did he even have a cell phone? I couldn't just call him. I needed to stay busy.

Lexi walked in with Caleb attached to her. He seemed to go from giddy in love to being filled with rage and worry.

"Where is Liam?" Caleb demanded.

"Gone." I said.

Cautiously, he asked, "Are you okay?"

I looked at him for a minute. Something was different about him too but it was a different kind of different. Did he know what Liam was? Did he know if Liam was okay? What If Caleb was one of the ones after me?

"What's going on?" Lexi asked concerned. Probably because of the looks Caleb and I were exchanging.

"Nothing." I smiled. "Do you want me to… go get some stuff from the store?" Code for do I need to give you two some privacy.

"Actually, I'm leaving soon. I don't want to keep you girls up too late. Lexi, I had a wonderful time." He kissed her hand and backed out towards the door, then gave me another glance. Lexi was on cloud nine, except she wasn't sure why Caleb didn't want to stay. She thought he was being gentlemanly. I, on the other hand, wasn't so sure about him anymore. Did he know more than I did? My head was spinning with questions and flashes. I'm not sure how, but I managed to go to sleep.

I woke up the next day to my phone ringing. At first I tried to press snooze, until I realized it wasn't my alarm clock. I answered sounding groggy.

"Alana, I've been trying to call. I haven't heard from you sweetie are you alright? Grandpa Joe said to give you some space, but I really just wanted to check on you. Are you coming home for Labor Day, hun? If so I want to go to the store. You don't have to come. If you have plans, that's fine. Sweetie are you there? Hello? I can't hear with this stupid phone." She didn't let me get two words in.

"Grandma, Grandma. I'm here." I said.

"You sound sick are you okay? Did I wake you?" She asked. I looked at the clock. It was almost noon. I needed to brake this habit of sleeping so late.

"Yeah, I'm sorry. I stayed out late with Lexi. We finally saw Beauty and the Beast."

"Oh how was it?" She asked. I hadn't noticed until just then that I spent most of my time thinking about Liam instead of the movie.

"It was amazing." I lied. Not that it wasn't, just that I didn't seem to get to watch much.

"Oh and yeah, I'm coming home. Sorry I haven't called or visited. I've been so busy."

"That's okay hun. I'm glad you're having fun. Is Lexi coming too? She asked. Grandma Hazel was almost just as much her grandmother as she was mine.

"No, her dad said something about renting a yacht and going somewhere tropical. She also mentioned shopping. So not this time. Just me." I said.

"Okay, well honey I hate to go but the oven is beeping. I'll go pick up some of the stuff you like. I love you and I'm so proud of you."

"I Love you too, oh and tell Papa Joe hi for me. I'm sure he's napping right about now."

I tried to get myself together. How was I supposed to pretend all was well and normal with everything that just happened? I didn't even know what just happened. I needed to know if Liam was okay. At first I was scared of him, then he annoyed me, now I just need to know that he is okay.

A few days went by. I tried to focus on school but I made a 70 on a quiz and an 80 on an essay. I have never made grades so low. So many things were happening. I had no idea what was going on with my own life anymore. I felt like I was constantly on the lookout. Were people still after me? Were they even people? Where was Liam? Caleb started hanging around more. He kept asking about Liam. I said he was probably busy with school. Lexi asked about him too, but she didn't seem as concerned.

We went to the movies again. Caleb bought both of our tickets and refreshments. He didn't seem to be taking advantage of Lexi like most guys did. I think that what made me like him. He felt like a friend. Loyal, almost. It felt good when the three of us hung out. Caleb liked to goof off a lot, but I could tell it was just because he liked to make people happy. Honestly, he was one of the most mature guys I had ever met. He seemed to understand my love for books and had a good grasp of history. He mentioned that his family has always been into history. He invited us to go to one of his football games, but it was on a Saturday and that would interfere with going home.

I began packing for my trip home. At least I would be safe there. Maybe I should leave a note for Liam if he comes here. No. that might be weird. It also felt weird going home without Lexi. Although, she went on vacations a lot. But most of the time she avoided her family. Still, it wasn't hard for her dad to persuade her. I'm just surprised she can peel herself away from Caleb. He is all she has talked about. She even told me she would cancel her vacation and stay here with Caleb. Apparently Caleb is a local. I convinced her to go on the trip. She has a family, she should spend time with them, no matter how imperfect they are.

I loaded my car and started the nearly two hour trip home. I put on my best playlist to try to distract me as I drove. There was a comfort pulling closer to my home town. I liked to pass the welcome sign and see the schools I went to, the church I attended, the places I worked and hung out. It also pained me sometimes, not all memories were good. Nothing compared to the feeling of pulling up to my grandparents' house though. It looked the same as it always has, except it looked like no one has mowed in a few weeks, or even months.

They lived in an older home. It was beautiful. It's a white house with a porch all around the front with a lot of valences and swings and rocking chairs. They love to garden so there are flowers all around the house. They have enough property for a garden around the side of the house that almost makes a maze. More so now that it seems to have grown over. It leads back to a pond and old willow tree with a swing. I started to feel bad. I'm normally the one who would mow and take care of the yard, but I've been away so much. I could tell they have been trying. I could see some spot that have been weeded and well maintained, but it's a large house and a large property.

I pulled in and parked my car. I would come out for the rest of my stuff, but first I just wanted to be home. I wanted to see my Grandma Hazel and Papa Joe. I walked up to the door and knocked. It was probably unlocked, and I had a key anyways, but I felt like knocking. I wanted to be invited in. Just as I heard the hand on the door about to open I felt a gush of wind and someone standing behind me. I looked over and it was Liam!

Chapter 15

LIAM

I didn't want to leave her, but I was in no shape to protect her like this. She had already seen me blink before, so there was no use pretending. I had to get out of there as quick as I could. I knew she would have questions. I didn't know if I would ever be able to answer them, but first I needed to be healed. I didn't know who I could trust. I couldn't go to Idris or Atticus. There was no way I would go to Baron for help. I blinked myself about a block from the sanctuary. It was dark outside and no one was around. I was hoping my window would still be open so I could fly in. I really wished blinking was an option. But it wasn't, and my window was closed. The only was in was through the front door.

I waited until I saw the right opportunity. The pain was worse than anything I had ever felt. I knew I was losing a lot of blood. If I was a human I would have died by now. I'm not sure what happens to Guardians. No one does. No one asks. I assume that we still exist on some form, maybe we are just sent back to the Father. Guardians weren't supposed to fear death, but I certainly wasn't ready to find out. I felt faint. It was something. I have never felt before. I could feel myself slipping away.

"Liam?" I heard. I looked up I was on the steps of the sanctuary. I must have kept walking and fallen over. I looked up and saw Justin. I've known him my whole life. He was the biggest Guardian I have ever seen. Even in human form he was nearly seven feet tall with muscles that barely fit in any normal clothes. When I first saw him as a child I was very intimidated. He was actually one of the nicest Angels I have ever met. He has was just and fair, but he had a gentleness and humor unlike anyone I had ever met. Anyone who would see him would think he was some twenty-nine year old giant. I used to joke and call him Lurch from some old TV show I heard about. He was one of the strongest angles in our area. Although, he wasn't the fastest. I could out fly him any day.

"Liam!" Justin said. I looked into his hazel eyes. I could tell he was concerned and confused. I'm not sure what Idris told the others about me, but it seemed like he was clueless.

"I need help." I said quickly. "But no one can know I was here." I said starring him dead in the eyes. I wasn't sure what he would do. I was worried about getting caught, but I was also worried about her. What if they came for her now?

I woke up in the Library. It was in the basement of the Cathedral. It's were we documented everything. I didn't see anyone around except for Justin. He stayed quiet. I could tell I wasn't all the way healed, but I felt good enough to fly and to fight if need be. I wasn't sure what to tell Justin. I started to open my mouth to talk to him.

"Liam, I don't need to know right now. I know you. You mess up sometimes, but you are pure of heart. I'm not sure what Idris has you doing, or if she even knows what you are doing but the less I know the better." He said.

"Where is Atticus?" I asked. He looked confused again, like he didn't know how to answer. "Justin, where is he?" I demanded.

"Gone. We don't know. No one can find him or sense him." He said.

"He's not with any of his missions?" I yelled. He shook his head. I immediately thought about Alana. I had to get back to her. There was no telling how long I had been out. She could be hurt, or worse. Thinking that gave me a feeling that tore at my stomach that matched the pain of the knife going through my stomach. I barely knew her, but I felt responsible for her. Maybe more than responsible. I liked being around her. She was good.

I blinked out of the sanctuary to her dorm. Luckily Lexi wasn't there. I didn't know how I would explain that. I still didn't know what I would tell Alana. It didn't matter she wasn't here. My thoughts went black. My whole body felt like it was on fire. I tried to push those thoughts from my mind. I had to focus on her. It wouldn't be too hard. It was easier to sense her than anyone else. I could pick up the connection quickly. I saw her in a car, I saw a house. She was going home. I looked at the calendar. It was Labor Day weekend. On Thursday in red ink was the word home with an exclamation mark. I collected myself. I saw her on the doorstep. I couldn't help it. I could have watched her from a distance, but a part of my longed to get to know her.

I blinked right next to her as her grandmother opened the door. I tried hard to ignore the look of shock, anger, and worry on Alana's face. It never ceased to amaze me how many emotions one person could feel at once. I was really good at reading emotions. I put on the biggest smile I could along with the most charming act I could muster to meet her family. There wasn't any reason I couldn't have a little fun with all of this.

Chapter 16

ALANA

What was he doing here? I was glad he was okay, but how could he just leave like that and show up now? I've been worried sick about him and he shows up here after days of not hearing anything and he's perfectly fine. Which just added to the list of questions I had ready for him. The only explanation I could think of was he had superpowers from another planet. Not only is he here, but he's standing in the doorway with me at my grandparents' house! What was I supposed to tell them? Obviously he liked watching me squirm. I just stood here trying to come up with what to say. How do I explain this boy standing here next to me?

Before I could say anything He held out his hand and said, "Hi, I'm Liam. I go to school with Alana. I hope you don't mind me tagging along. She always talks about home, and I guess I didn't have anywhere else to go for the holiday, so here I am. It's so good to finally meet you and to see where Laney here grew up."

Oh that turd! I could punch him right in the face every time he called me Laney! And what would my grandparents think of this? Me bringing a boy home. Clearly they would read too much into it. I hoped they wouldn't be disappointed in me. On the contrary, Grandma Hazels face light up. Perfect. Then Bucky came running up to me. His white fur was covered in dirt and grass. He must have been playing outside. He looked like he was going to run me over, well run my feet over, but he stopped and looked up at Liam. He sat down and just looked at him. No barking, no jumping, to biting. Bucky seemed to be smiling at him, if dogs could smile and right then I believed Bucky could. Great even the dog likes him.

"Oh, I don't mean to intrude. I guess we should have called first. As soon as we get Alana settled in I was going to try to find a place to stay. I hope you don't think I just showed up planning to stay in your house." He said apologetically as he bent down to pet Bucky. At least this time he didn't call me Laney.

Again, before I could even say a word Grandma Hazel chimed in. "Oh no, we wouldn't have that. Alana rarely brings friends from school, and certainly not a boyfriend..." Oh, that word. She did not think we were together did she? Of course she did. That explains why her face light up. "No friend of Alana is going to sleep in any old hotel room. We have plenty of room here." She stopped. "In the guest room." She said slowly looking at me a little concerned. Oh God! She thought we might be sleeping together! I'm pretty sure fire was shooting through my ears right now. Yes, I had questions for Liam. Yes, I was worried about him. And, yes, I'm curious about him, but this was way out of line!

"Oh no, really I couldn't intrude. I know you will want to catch up with Alana." He said.

"Oh don't be silly sweetie. We would love to have you. We have plenty of room. This house is a bit old, but it has a lot of room." She seemed a little embarrassed. "I'm sorry about the yard. I tried to get the house looking good, it's just been..."

Liam interrupted and said "You have a lovely home." She smiled and seemed very pleased.

"Is that our little Laney I hear?" Croaked Papa Joe. If everyone could just chill with the 'Laney' thing, that would be great. I could tell he had a hard time getting up. He must have been laying in his recliner. Bucky ran back to Grandpa Joe like that little ten pound dog was going to help my grandfather out of the recliner. I walked up and gave him a big hug and a kiss on the cheek. I couldn't help but notice that his face seemed a little paler and his eyes seemed to droop a little more than usual. It worried me. He smiled, then looked past me to Liam. I saw his eyebrow raise. Grandma Hazel gladly introduced 'my boyfriend' Liam. Liam didn't even hold out his hand. Which was probably a good thing. Papa Joe was a big teddy bear, but he liked to appear tough. I don't imagine he would have taken his hand anyways. I think right about now he's trying to remember where he put his rifle. The thought almost made me laugh. Liam almost looked scared as if he could read Papa Joes mind. I bit my lip to keep from smiling. Liam saw me and gave me a look.

It was kind of quiet for a minute, and I said, "Well I guess I should get my bags."

"No, don't worry babe. I'll get them. You sit down and visit with your grandparents." Liam said.

Did he really just call me babe? Babe, like we've known each other more than just a few weeks. My head was spinning. I just wanted to go to my room.

"Actually, I think I'm going to… freshen up in my room first. It felt like a long drive and I'm a little tired." I said.

"Well, be down for dinner it will be ready in about thirty minutes, and I made dessert. Oh. And when were done I laid out your favorite game, the four of us could play. That would be fun huh? Unless, maybe you would prefer to do something else? I don't want to pressure you, but you don't know the real Alana until you have played a round or two of Uno with her." Grandma Hazel smiled.

"Uno?" Liam asked.

"Cards." I replied, still curious to why he didn't seem to know anything about anything.

"I'm not sure if I have ever played, but I'm a quick learner." Liam smiled.

I went to my room while Liam went to go get my bags from the car. He brought them to my room and started to come in, but I shut the door in his face. I felt bad. I mean, he almost died for me. It was just weird him being here. I opened the door again, "Liam?" I whispered. He came back and kept his distance. "I'm sorry. It's just… I don't know where to start. I don't know anything about you." I said.

"It's okay. I don't know if I can answer your questions. I'm sorry I just took off. You're still in danger. Maybe more so than before. I don't mean to impose, but I can't leave you alone." He said. We both just kind of stood there looking at each other as if we both had questions that neither of us knew how to ask or how to answer.

"Dinner's ready!" Grandma Hazel yelled from downstairs, which got Bucky started on a barking spree. We both went down. I kept staring at him. I couldn't get out of my mind what I had seen the other night. What was he? I watched as he ate. He seemed to enjoy everything, but everything seemed new to him. I stayed out of most of the conversation. Grandma Hazel had a million questions for him. She asked where he was from and he said he was born near Huntsville. She asked about his parents and he paused for a minute and said his father left before he was born and his mother died. I felt a familiar pain sneak up on me. So, he did have parents. Maybe he was more normal than I thought. I could tell she felt bad for asking, and without even looking I could sense her looking at me. They asked what he did. He answered slowly, but said he was an intern. He said he liked to help people. Grandma Hazel asked if he was studying medicine. He looked conflicted for a second and said that he was. I knew it was a lie, but the intern part seemed real. Intern for who? He kept changing the subject and asking about them, and about me. Grandma Hazel gloated on everything I had ever done. She talked about my cheerleading days, my grades and perfect attendances, all of my awards, all of the clubs and sports I had ever been in. She even brought up the time I played a banana in a school play about nutrition. I turned a little red. My life must sound so boring compared to his.

After dinner Liam offered to help clean up, but Grandma Hazel told him to go ahead and find a spot in the living room so I could teach him the rules of Uno before we started our big tournament. Papa Joe had been quiet for most of the evening. It seemed to me like he was in pain. I knew he was trying to hide it. Liam seemed to notice too. It didn't take long to teach him the rules and my grandmother was still cleaning up. I went in to help her, but told Liam to stay behind. There was no since in him offering again. He's a guest to my grandmother. Which meant she would try to fatten him up and send him home without lifting a finger off of his seemingly strong hands. I got distracted thinking about his hands and how they led to all of his strong muscles. I thought about the nights where he had protected me. I got lost in the questions again. How could he seem so inhuman?

Before I knew it we were done. Even Bucky was done. I saw him lying in the corner asleep next to Grandpa Joe just listening to his comforting voice. When I walked in I noticed Papa Joe telling old war stories to Liam. Only, this time they weren't horror stories and he wasn't trying to hold back. Instead he was laughing and telling him about his days as a recruit and all of the trouble he got into. I hadn't seen that spark in his eyes in a long time. For the first time, I felt grateful for Liam being here. We gathered around the coffee table to play cards.

Papa Joe sat in his old worn out blue recliner, Grandma Hazel sat in her velvet old style chair next to his. I took my place on the floor. I liked the room and freedom it gave me. I guess I did get a little competitive. Normally Lexi was here playing with me. She wasn't one who really like to hang out with old people or play cards, but she never complained. I think she liked the normalcy it gave her. Also, I think she just liked to make me laugh.

Liam sat next to me and we began the game.

Chapter 17

LIAM

It felt nice being here. I had never been a part of anything like this. The closest thing to family that I had ever seen was what I observed, and whatever family type thing we had at the sanctuary. It was nice to sit down, relax, and laugh. I felt bad because once I got a hang of the game it was impossible for me to loose. I could read people so well, especially Alana. She got really into the game. It was easy to tell when she had a good hand, and what kind of card she was about to play. She seemed so mad to lose. It seemed strange to me to see someone get into a meaningless game. Nothing about this game would affect her life at all. It was just for fun. All the same, it seemed to matter to her. I decided to let her win a few hands. I think she knew I was letting her win, but she seemed pleased either way.

I hadn't realized how long we had been playing until the clock started to chime and her grandparents looked at each other. They both said they were tired and going to bed. Grandma hazel looked at Alana and kissed her forehead. She whispered to her to not stay up to late. I knew they felt uneasy about leaving us. I told them I would probably be heading to be soon too. Bucky slowly scampered off behind them, but not before nudging Alana with his wet puppy nose.

"What tired already?" Alana joked. I think she was aware that I didn't tire easily. I didn't answer. I got up and started looking, even studying their house. It seemed to be filled with useless clutter, but I had a sense that all this clutter was meaningful to them. There were pictures everywhere, and shelves filled with books. There were pots of flowers even in the house. It was neat and tidy, but it definitely looked lived in and worn through the years. Alana just watched as I carefully examined the house. This house felt so warm. It was as if I could see memories and lifetimes all taking place at one time in one place.

I didn't know how long she planned to stay up and watch me, and I wasn't sure why she wasn't asking me anything. "I should go to bed." I said. She was standing in the doorway or the hall. I walked up to her, smiled and nodded my head. "Good night." I said. She just tilted her head and watched me walk to my room. I heard her walk into her room shortly after and shut her door. I couldn't sleep. It wasn't really necessary to sleep and I certainly didn't want to. I kept thinking about Alana. I wondered about her life growing up. She had never mentioned her parents and I never thought to ask. I saw the look on her face when I said my mom had died. Not only that I found myself wondering what her favorite movie was, her favorite food, her favorite song. Atticus would surely know all of these things. Mostly I thought about Atticus. It wasn't like him to disappear and leave a mission, especially one in so much trouble. What had happened to him?

The next morning I heard Alana's grandmother working in the kitchen. I could tell she was cooking breakfast. I couldn't sense if Alana was up or not, which probably meant she was still asleep. I couldn't hear Grandpa Joe either. I guessed that he was still sleeping. I figured

I might as well make my way from the room. I hadn't slept so I didn't actually need to clean up the room. I found the bathroom and splashed some water on my face. I still looked every bit the same as I had the day before, but I needed to look like I slept and woke up. I figured washing my face would make it look like I tried to look better, even if I didn't need it. I heard Alana get up and out of bed. I decided it might be awkward if I was too close to her room when she woke up so I went downstairs to the kitchen.

"Oh, Good morning Hun." Hazel said cheerfully. I gave her my best smile and told her good morning. The small dog came up to me and started wagging his small tail, but there were a few scraps on the floor and he was more interested in them. Hazel asked how I slept, I hated to lie but I wasn't sure what to say. Instead, I told her that the bed was comfortable. I heard Alana coming down the stairs. She looked natural, but she seemed to put a little effort into looking nice this morning. I guess for her grandparents. I could see her hair was brushed, she had a bit of perfume on, and I could tell she was wearing a little makeup.

"Hi." She said.

"Hi." I replied.

Hazel broke the silence. "I need to take your grandfather to go get his medicine today. It's a bit out of town and might take a while. Instead of being cooped up here all day, why don't you take Liam around the town and show him around." She offered.

"Oh, I didn't realize you needed to go anywhere. I could come with you." Alana said. Hazel told her not to worry, that it would be a boring trip that would probably take way longer than necessary. I could sense Alana's worry.

"I'd love that." I said, hoping to take her mind off of it. That, and I'm pretty sure Alana got her stubbornness from Hazel. I wanted to skip the back and forth they were about to have. "So, where are you going to take me?" I asked.

"Well, I need to get ready first." Alana said.

"Ready, your hair is perfect, you're dressed, and you're clearly already wearing makeup." Hazel snickered as if she was making fun of Alana. Alana gave her a fierce look. I seriously thought she was going to stick her tongue out at her.

"Well, we don't have much here. We have a park, a movie theater, a Walmart, lots of places to eat. That's about it." She said.

"Oh a Wal-Mart" I joked.

"Shut up.' She hissed.

"The park sounds nice." I added.

She went back upstairs to get dressed. Her hair seemed to have a natural wave to it that curled around the ends and her face when it was humid outside. She wore simple shorts and a loose shirt. She looked nice. I wasn't sure why. It was a very plain outfit, but she made it look good. For a moment I felt self-conscious about what I was wearing. I was wearing my usual faded blue jeans and a black shirt. She drove. It felt weird sitting in the passenger seat. There was something different about her. She seemed so comfortable. She threw on some big sunglasses that made her face look really small. She turned on the radio to some new music that I had never heard. I don't know if she realized it, but she was singing along. This was the happiest that I had ever seen her. We pulled up to the park. She got out and waited for me.

"So, this is it. It's not much." There was a walking trail, a tennis court, and volleyball court, a place for basketball, a spot with picnic tables, a playground, and a pond with a bridge. The pond was pretty dirty and the park was nearly empty. She started walking over to the swings and sat on one. I knew she had a lot on her mind. I sat next to her and we started swinging. Neither of us really said anything.

"You want to go for a walk?" I asked. She nodded. We started walking towards the pond she stood on the bridge and watched the ducks.

"We used to come out here and feed the ducks when I was little." She said. I couldn't tell if I was picking up happy emotions or sad emotions. She leaned over and glared at the water. She seemed to see something in the reflection. She turned to look at me and her hair was in her face. I reached up and gentle tucked it behind her ear. She didn't even flinch when I touch her. She felt so warm. My hand stayed there a little longer than I meant it to. It felt like a magnet being pulled towards her. There were some flowers nearby. They were the same flowers from the garden at the safe house. I picked one and put it in her hair I smiled and laughed. I have no idea why I laughed. It just came out. She laughed too. The way her lips curled into a smile made my stomach feel sick, which I didn't understand. I couldn't be sick. She leaned her head over towards the car, smiled again, and said come on.

"Where are we going?" I acquired. She gave me a funny little squint, pursed her lips together into a mischievous smile, and scrunched her nose. I followed. We got in the car. I wasn't sure where we were going. We pulled up to a store. It was Wal-Mart. I tried hard not to laugh. Was she serious?

"Come on!" She yelled.

"Are we going shopping?' I yelled back.

"Nope"

"So… what are we doing?" I asked.

"It's a small town we make do." She ran in the store almost skipping. She found a spot and told me to wait there. I waited for a long time I started to get worried. Just as I decided to go look for her she immerged. She was wearing a grandma nightgown over her clothes, a grandma wig, a ridiculously large purse, with a matching large hat. I busted out into laughter right then and there. I'm not even sure I had ever heard myself laugh in that way. I mean, I've laughed before but this was different. "Your turn." She said.

"I don't get it." I said.

"There aren't any rules. Just find something funny and come back and surprise me." I had no idea what to do. I hadn't ever even been in a Wal-Mart, but hey had just about everything here. How was I supposed to surprise her and make her laugh? I saw the bike section. I had never ridden a bike, but I could fly. How hard can riding a bike be. I got the smallest one they had, probably for toddlers. It was pink with a bell and fringe stuff coming out of the handles. I stepped over it and sat down. It felt very uncomfortable. I finally got it going and managed to drive it over to her but when I got close enough I bumped into a rack of sunglasses and half of them fell on the floor. It worked. She was laughing. I felt like an idiot though.

"Come on let's get some ice-cream." She said. I had imagined that this is what she and Lexi did in their spare time. When we got to the line I looked puzzled. She asked what was wrong. I told her I didn't have any money. She seemed to not be too surprised. She paid for both of ours and she didn't seem to mind. I have never felt so vulnerable before. I'm used to having all of this power and now I can't even buy my own ice-cream.

When we got home it was late. We had spent all day driving around. I still wasn't sure why she hadn't asked me any questions. We ate dinner, her grandparents went to bed, and I walked her to her room. She let me in. I looked around. It looked very her. She had a book shelf with more books than any young girl would want to read. She had completely made this space her own. I noticed she had a large window looking out to the garden. It reminded me of my window at the sanctuary.

There were pictures everywhere. She liked to make colleges on the walls. Mostly the pictures were of her and Lexi. There were a few other people I didn't recognize and her grandparents. There was one particular photo by her bed that she glanced at. I slowly walked over and held it up. My head started to spin with disbelief and I flash backed to my very first mission along with Atticus.

Atticus nodded at me to come. I wasn't used to flying back then. He talk me to follow my scenes. I tried, but was still too nervous. Instead I followed him. Atticus was large, even for a Guardian. He has always seemed so serious. He's the kind of guy that doesn't break the rules. Maybe that's why Idris picked him to be my mentor. When we arrived there was a small car flipped over on its side. It was as if another car ran them off the road. It was an especially dark night, filled with rain and storms. There were two Free Wills (Missions) in the car. Atticus appeared in human form and tried to pull the woman from the vehicle. The memory was still so fresh to me. I did as well and went to the man. I was nervous because I was just learning to heal. I eagerly searched Atticus' face. There was a solemn look on his face. Guardians have brought people back before.

The Heavenly sky seemed to part. It was beautiful. When I realized what was happening I began to plead Atticus to let it stop. I saw Angels ascend from above and come to the couple. This was my first mission. I didn't want to fail. Atticus saw the look on my face. He knew what I was thinking. He grabbed me and made me focus on him. He said the mission wasn't a fail. This was just how it had to be. I looked passed him. I saw these beautiful lights come out of the couple in the car. They still looked like themselves. Not quite a human, but not quite an angel. They looked at each other, then at the sky. It was hard to read their faces. Their faces were riddled with contradiction. Sadness gloomed through their eyes, but so did great joy and peace. I guess that's what kept me going. The peace in their faces. But, that didn't stop me from getting in trouble. I didn't necessarily disobey, but I didn't comply either. For any other guardian that would be a direct disobedience. For me, it was just another screw up.

"Liam?" Alana asked. She could see shock written on my face.

"Your parents?" I ask quietly. She gave a forced smile and nodded once. I could see tears welling up in her eyes until one felon her check. It pained me to see her upset. It also made me outraged to know that if I had saved her parents she wouldn't feel this way right now. Without hesitation I wiped her tear from her cheek and tucked her hair behind her ear. I stared into her eye. I started to think how hard it must have been for her parent to leave her behind. It was late. I told her good night and turned around and went to my room.

All night I thought about her parents it was my fault they weren't her, and it was my fault that she was in trouble now. I thought back about everything I knew about Alana. She didn't deserve so much heartache. If the father loved her so much, why had he allowed this to happen to her? I hated being cooped up in this room. I went out to walk the garden. I needed to clear my head.

Chapter 18

ALANA

I couldn't sleep. Every time I closed my eyes I would either think of my parents, or flash back to the night those men attacked me, or I'd flash back to the night Liam got hurt. Why was he trying to protect me? And, why was no one there to protect them? I had spent all night tossing and turning. The sun was starting to come up. I went to my window and saw Liam in the garden sitting on a bench. I could swear the dew around him formed some sort of shape. It was like it didn't touch him, but something around him. He looked magical. The suns glow bounced and reflected off of his long blond curls. He held his head in his hands. I don't think he had slept all night either. I wasn't even sure if he slept in general. I don't know why I haven't confronted him. Maybe I wasn't sure I would believe him, or maybe I was afraid that I would believe him. I untwisted my hair from its bun on top on my head so that it would twist in long curls and I found a cotton sun dress that was easy to throw on. I didn't even worry about putting on shoes. I went outside.

There was dew everywhere and the air was very hot and humid. My grandparents had allowed the garden to grow over and it was hard to see passed the hedges. It made sort of a small maze to the garden. When I got outside he wasn't on the bench anymore. He must have moved further into the garden. I followed the stone path. Something about it seemed unreal. Like a dream. I could feel the cold stone under my feet as I tip toed further. I saw him standing by our willow tree by the pond looking out. He turned towards me and smiled. It was the soft sweet smile that allowed for his dimple to kiss his cheek. The wind blew slightly brushing my hair from my face. The way he smiled make we think he knew the wind was going to blow. I walked up to him.

He was really quiet and I wanted to break the silence so I pretended to push him in to the pond. I knew I couldn't push him in. He would be too strong, but when I pushed him he didn't even budge. He didn't even use any effort. He laughed at me which made me feel dumb.

"What? Can't swim?" I said.

"I don't know. I've never tried." I must have given him the most puzzling look. I looked down and noticed he was holding a flower. It was just like the other two. He handed it to me. I took it in my hands. When I did, our hands brushed. Something about his skin. It seemed alive. Every time I touched him it was like an energy vibrating off of him onto me. I sat down on the swing that was tied to a far branch from the willow tree. He sat beside me but facing the other direction so we were facing each other. I twirled my bare toes into the ground while one arm looped around the swings and the other held the flower. I hadn't notice but the sun was fading away. It wasn't night, the clouds were just covering it. It started to get windier. My hair started blowing every which direction. He reached up and tucked my hair behind my ear. Every time he did this it felt like a shock of electricity moving through my body from my head to my feet. We locked gazes. His eye looked like they had seen the universe. There was so much mystery in them, but so much light as well.

His hand was still on my face when I felt a few water droplets hitting my cheeks. In a flash it started pouring rain. It was more rain that I had ever seen, but the sun seemed to be shining through the rain. We both ran to take cover under the center of the willow tree, hoping it would shield us from the sudden down pour. He looked worried. Almost sorry, as if he had caused it. I felt like my whole body was radiating with life. I couldn't help but to laugh. I ran out into the rain and twirled around. I wanted to be in the rain. It felt like a part of him. My hair was dripping and my dress was soaked. My feet were covered in mud. It felt good. When I stopped spinning I looked over at him. He seemed puzzled. He smiled and slowly walked towards me.

Everything seemed like it was happening in slow motion. Each drop of water was illuminated by the sun's rays. Again, I saw it. It was like a window behind him. Something was glistening in the rain. It seemed like gold specks floating around. The rain seemed to be stopped around him. He seemed taller, bigger. I had to keep blinking. It was like waking from a dream. So fuzzy I couldn't make out. There was more to him. I knew it.

We were close now. He put his hand on my face. With it came a chill of warmth and electricity fly through me. It felt both warm and cold at the same time. I couldn't take my eyes off of him. With each passing second he seemed to get closer and closer. Finally he leaned in. I could feel his breath on my face. I closed my eyes and our lips met. It was the softest, yet strongest kiss I have ever experienced. He felt like a silk statue. He was firm and strong, but soft as silk. When he finally leaned away and I opened my eyes. I saw him gazing at me with such intensity. I wanted to be with him, to be close to him. I felt like a charged magnet. The closer we were the stronger the pull was. I felt giddy. I had so much energy rushing through my body. I laughed and spun around again, but he stopped me mid spin and firmly pulled me close to him pressing his lips to mine and letting them separate. The kiss felt so passionate. I wanted to stay there forever. His strong arms wrapped around me, holding me close. His lips intertwined with mine. He slowly let go and looked at me. His eyes seemed to ask if I was okay. If it was okay that we had kissed. It was more than okay.

As I looked into his eyes I felt like I wanted to know him. Know everything about him. "Let me see you." I said. He looked confused.

"I haven't gone anywhere." He replied.

"No, I want to see the real you." I begged.

"It's not a good idea."

"Please." I said reaching up to touch his face. He grabbed my hand and stepped back. He looked at me, then closed his eyes. He seemed to disappear, but I could still feel my hand in his. I kept blinking. The water from the rain seemed to move around him, but he didn't seem to be there. There was that same shimmer I saw before. A form started to take place, but it seemed to be transparent. The first thing I saw was his eyes. It was like I was looking at an old photograph that had captures two images. There was the dominant one. The garden, with nothing but me. The, there was this other being. The longer I stared, the clearer he became. He was much larger than before. He had wings. I think they were wings. Not like bird's wings. These didn't seem to have a real shape. It looked both like a spider web and a shield. He was beautiful. I couldn't peel my eyes from him. I couldn't speak. I didn't want to. I knew that I had never seen anything so beautiful, and I never would again.

My eyes wanted to drink every ounce of him. I'm not sure how long we stood there just starring at each other, but eventually he turned about. He seemed alarmed. His glow turned from gold to a red tent. Like the sun was burning brighter than I had ever seen. The rain stopped and he was gone. I called out to him. I didn't know where he went. I didn't know why he went.

Chapter 19

LIAM

I had never felt anything like this before. The longer I stayed as a human the more I gave into it, the more I craved the things around me. The people around me. Her, mostly. I felt lost in everything. Lost in her, and I wanted to be lost in her completely. I could sense her coming behind me. I felt such an energy. A nervousness. I wasn't sure I could face her. I wasn't sure if I wanted to run away from her, or hold her and never let go. Not just to protect her, but because I wanted to feel her embrace. I got up and started walking. I slowly walked a stone path through what looked like a small maze. The hedges and vines were so overgrown, it looked like the garden was a paradise. I made my way to a swing tied to an old willow tree. It hung from a branch that was far from the trunk. It overlooked a small pond. I could imagine her swinging on this tree as a child. I could imagine her mother pushing her here. She walked up behind me and seemed to be trying to push me in to the pond. I was confused at why until I saw her sweet joking smile. She had no idea what I was feeling inside, feeling for her.

I think she knew she wouldn't be strong enough to push me in. When she put her hands on me, I felt like nothing I had ever felt before. She looked so natural, but she radiated beauty. I have traveled the world and seen great beauty, but nothing compared to this. Her hair feel effortlessly in the wind. It was tangled and loose, which made it seem wild like a fire in a jungle. She was wearing a beautiful sun dress that blew as the wind blew, and her feet were bare. I swore I had never seen such beautiful feet. That seemed weird to think, but everything about her as radiant. She made her way over to the swing to sit down. She twirled her feet in the dirt looking down then pierced me with her eyes. I moved closer and sat beside her. There was just enough room. I sat facing the other way so I could look into her eyes. I could tell I was making the wind pick up a bit. Her hair started to blow in her face and the sight of her made me feel like I was melting. Rain started to fall, just a sprinkling mist. It kissed her cheeks. I couldn't help but to feel jealous of the rain. My hand glided to her face. I wiped away the rain from her face. I ran my hands through her hair and tucked it behind her ear. I could smell her shampoo as her hair gently fell behind her shoulder. The smell sent me into a frenzy. Rain started to pour. I didn't want her to get wet. We ran to the tree trunk because it was closer than the house. The old willow tree helped to shield some of the rain, but it seeped through the leaves and soaked her all over. I thought about using my wings to shield the rain from her, no matter how much I tried to calm the rain down, I couldn't. I was going to reach out to her but she ran off. I couldn't help but to think I scared her off, that I had done something wrong. I saw her stand out in the rain. She looked right at me then started to twirl and spin. It was a sight to behold. I was nearly afraid that I would cause a hurricane. 'Control yourself' I thought.

I started walking towards her like I had no choice. I have never felt so powerless. She stopped and stared at me. My hand caressed her face.

I felt like I was being pulled towards her, like I was being sucked in by a black hole. She was looking at me, almost looking right through me to my core. I leaned in and our lips met. I felt both like a raging fire, and a calm leaf floating on a pond. I couldn't believe she let me kiss her. She didn't pull away. She didn't seem afraid. I tried to catch on to what she was feeling. I felt electricity jolt through my body. I pulled away and looked at her. I hoped I hadn't hurt her. Why did she feel like she was on fire? But, as I looked in her eyes I knew she was feeling the same way I was. I wanted to lean in again but she spun around again. Crazy girl. I wanted her, I needed her. I didn't know why she was spinning in the rain. I grabbed her by her shoulders, placed one hand behind her head and pulled her close to me and pressed my lips on hers once again. My other arm wrapped around her waist. I pulled her as close as I could. I felt like her kiss could set me on fire. I felt my wings flair out behind me, but I know she wouldn't see them no matter what I did. It took everything in me to pull away. I studied her face. I needed to know that it was okay. Okay to love her. I needed to know she felt the same way about me.

She reached up and touched my face. She whispered to me that she wanted to know me, but she did know me. She knew more about me than anyone had my entire existence. Suddenly, I knew what she meant. I had barely thought about being an angel this entire weekend. All I have thought about was her. I wasn't sure if she would even see my wings, or if I wanted her to. At the moment I wanted nothing to do with being an Angel. I could see the curiosity and desperation in her face. I knew it would be a bad idea, but I wanted her to see all of me. I transformed. I could tell she couldn't see me. The only way she knew I was still there was because I was still touching her hand. The rain started to let up. It was still raining hair, but it was falling slower and lighter now. I watched her staring in to this empty hole where she knew

I was standing. Suddenly it was like her face light up. Her eyes looked right into mine. She stared into them for a while then they trailed to the span of my wings and the height of my body. Her eyes met mine again. Neither of us said anything. We stood there in silence soaking each other in.

Suddenly I felt another presence. Someone was watching us. I looked over and saw a blur behind the bushes. I knew it wasn't her grandparents. The fear crept back into me. I had forgotten all about the danger on her life, Atticus missing, the demons hunting us both. So many thoughts swarmed my mind. I had to follow him. I had to track him down. I flew after him. I couldn't keep up, he was too far gone. I was so frustrated that I kept going. I had traveled all the way to the ocean and stood on the water. Reality slapped me in the face. What had I done? She's a human. I can't have her. I had done the same thing to her that my father did to my mother. I took advantage of her, because I wanted her. I have always been impulsive. It was a side of myself I hated. I had to get back to the sanctuary. I needed Atticus. I had forgotten he was missing. Just then, horror struck me. I had left her. I was so busy chasing after the shadowy figure, so busy fighting with myself that I hadn't realized that I just left her alone and unprotected. I tried to focus in on her. She should still be at her grandparents. I wasn't sure. It was harder to tap into my powers. My mind was flooded with thoughts and fears that I couldn't block out. I felt weak. I realized that I hadn't fully healed, nor have I rested since the attack. I tried to blink back to her grandparents' house, but couldn't find the focus. I kept blinking all over the world. I couldn't get it right. The Angier I got, the harder it was to blink. There was lightning all around me. I tried to sense her but I couldn't.

Chapter 20

ALANA

I don't know where he went. The weather cleared up instantly. The rain was gone, although the sun never seemed to have stopped shining. I have never seen the sun shine so bright during rain before. It almost seemed like it didn't surprise me that he could disappear, what surprised me is that he did. I felt a sudden panic. What if someone had come for me? What if he was hurt again? I didn't know what to do. I just knew I had to do something. I couldn't stay here. He had said he was from Huntsville. I had to go back to school. But, he wouldn't be at school. Where would he be? I have heard him mention a statuary, I don't know if he meant church or safe place. Safe place, that reminds me. What if he is there? That house he took me to. That could be his sanctuary. He acted weird there. I wasn't sure if that was where he would be, but I had to find him. I had to make sure he was alright.

I didn't know what to tell my grandparents. I lied and said Liam had to get back home for an emergency. I told them he was able to get a ride back, but I wanted to say good bye. I packed my things and hugged them both. It wasn't until I said goodbye to Grandpa Joe that I realized something was different about him, he seemed better. I don't know what Liam was, but I know he had something to do with it. I drove back as quickly as I could. I couldn't quite remember where the house was but I found the road that lead away from town that had had come back on. I started to notice things that looked familiar. It didn't take long to see the old black iron gate with stone walls. I parked outside the gate and squeezed in the entrance of the gate like I had before. I ran to the house. The door was hard to open, but I finally got it open. I searched the house but couldn't find him. Maybe there was a clue here. I started to enter each room. It felt like a ghost house. It seemed creepier now, than it had when I woke up here. I'm not sure how that was even possible.

I found a picture in a frame. It was of a woman. She had jet black hair and a soft glowing smile. She was pregnant and holding her belly. The way she looked at the camera, or the person holding the camera was illuminating. She was in love. There was something about her eyes. I dusted the picture frame off with the bottom of my dress that I didn't realize I was still wearing. They were his eyes. This was his mom. This must be his house. What had happened to his mom? If he had a mom, that meant he had a dad. He mentioned that his mother died and his father had left them both, but how could he leave them. This woman was more beautiful than I had ever seen and appeared to be madly in love with the person behind the camera.

I began to feel more and more curious about this boy that I had barely know. This mysterious boy I had just met nearly a month ago. I had fallen completely and madly in love with him, but I knew so little about him. At the same time, I felt like I knew him so well. I heard something. It scared me and I dropped the picture frame. I bent over to pick it up. When I stood up I was face to face with another angel. He looked like Liam had looked. I could barely see him. I think if I hadn't believed he was there I wouldn't have seen him at all. Before I could speak I felt a wave of blackness rushing over me again. Oh no. Not this again.

It was quiet. I didn't know where I was. I struggled to open my eyes. I couldn't at first. I felt as if I were paralyzed.

"Where is Liam?" I heard. I didn't recognize the voice.

"I don't know." I mumbled.

"I need to know where he is." Someone yelled.

I peeled my eyes open. I felt like I weighted a million pounds. Everything on my body felt heavy, especially my eyelids. I strained to see who was speaking to me. As I focused my eyes I saw a figure, a man, walk towards a door and then leave. I was alone now, but I couldn't move I left like someone had laid bricks on my body. It was nearly impossible to open my eyes, or to speak. I was tied to a chair and couldn't hold my own head up. I knew where I was. Well, not really where. But I knew that THEY had found me.

Chapter 21

LIAM

My first thought was to go back to the sanctuary. They couldn't help me, Idris wouldn't let them. There would be nothing I could do to convince her to help. We kept the rules, so much so they we honestly didn't interfere with the demons and were unaware of their whereabouts. I might could hunt down a demon or a vampire and torture them, but I'm doubtful that would work. Most likely, it would be a waste of time. I didn't like where my mind was headed. There would be one person who could track Alana. A wolf. I dreaded to think of asking a wolf for help, but the longer I waited, the less likely I would be to see her again. I didn't know where he was, but I remembered he played football for the college. It should be time for practice. I blinked towards the stadium and, still in Angel form, I stood near to him. I knew he would be able to sense me. I'm not exactly sure if they can see us, or just sense us, but I could tell he knew I was close. He pretended to be sick and limped towards the locker room alone.

"So it's you." Caleb seemed tense. I clenched my jaw. I hated asking a wolf for help. I hated asking anyone for help.

"Alana needs your help." I said. Before he could even take a breath he charged at me with great strength. I knew he would be stronger than a human, especially since it would be a full moon that night.

"What did you do Nephilim?" He yelled pushing me against the lockers with his forearm across my neck and the other one pushing it in further. It didn't hurt me, but he was strong enough that it didn't feel good either.

"She was taken." I said. He looked angry and confused.

"Taken, what do you mean taken? Taken by who?" he asked desperately. The desperation sent a fire through me. I could hear the voices and footsteps of the other players and coaches coming.

"We should talk elsewhere. We need to leave." He tried to put more pressure on my neck, but I blinked us out and backup up. We were back at the house that I had kept Alana. I flew up to the balcony so he couldn't catch me, quickly at least.

Something felt off. Someone had been here. I looked around and everything seemed in its place, except a table looked like it had been recently dusted and there was broken glass on the floor. I picked up the object that had broken. It was a picture of a woman. A very beautiful woman with black hair. I almost lost my breath at how beautiful she was. I knew it must have been my mother. I know this is where Abner took her and kept her, but why did he have her picture here? Then I thought, why was it broken on the ground? It wasn't like this before. I know I didn't have time to look around, but someone had wiped the dust away from this picture. It must have been Alana. "Alana!" I yelled rushing from room to room trying to find her. Maybe she came here. Maybe she was safe. Nothing. I saw Caleb slowly walk in behind me. He was taking in the whole scene.

"She's been here. I can smell her." He said. "There's a recent scent." He paused and glared at me, "And an older one."

"I took her here to be safe." I explained.

"Well it doesn't seem to have worked did it? Why was she in trouble?" He asked, well, more like demanded. I didn't quite know what to say. I didn't know how to answer. It was my fault. I tried to explain that they were after her to get to me, but that didn't make it sound any better. Caleb looked furious. "So you want me to find her? Why don't you go get her?" He asked. I had to explain that we actually didn't even know where the fallen kept their hideout. He looked at me like I was crazy and asked if I was kidding. He was silent for a minute. "So you want me to track her? Then what? Do you have an army to go recue her? Or is it just you?"

"I will get her!" I yelled.

"Alone?" He yelled back.

"You can't go in there alone."

He was right. I needed to tell Idris what had happened. No matter what. Maybe there was something she could do to help. They took an innocent. I couldn't risk bringing Caleb to the sanctuary. I told him to start sniffing around to find Alana. I flew to the sanctuary. I almost flew right into those big golden eyes. Idris must have known I was coming. It appeared that she was waiting for me. For a second I lost my breath. I have never seen her look so intimidating. I paused for a moment, thinking she would say something. Instead, she stood there staring so intensely it was as if she was staring into my soul. I've rarely left fear in my life, and I wasn't sure why, but I was feeling it now. I began to explain what was going on. I started with the fact that I snuck out and broke territory law, on accident. But that didn't matter. I explained how I had been tailing Alana, but left out the whole kidnapping part. I also left out the part about her grandparent's garden. She knew I was keeping something back. There was no actual proof that I had done anything beyond breaking territory. For that, we are not going against the Father, just the region. The consequence was sometimes up to the fallen, or the guardian would be relocated. It wasn't a serious enough offence to lose your wings, and I of course was treated differently anyways. Kissing Alana though, that was serious.

I went back to that moment in my mind. Kissing her. Holding her in my arms. This girl with fiery red hair, blushed cheeks, and soft pink lips. I wanted so bad to hold her again, to be with her. But, more than that, I just wanted her safe. Even if that meant never holding her again.

She told me that I was no longer allowed in the sanctuary, and if I did anything else she would takes my wings. She had threatened to do so before, but never as serious as this. Then she pushed me away. Not with her hands. I mean with a force. A shocking wind pushed me several blocks from the sanctuary. I flew around until I found Caleb. Only. He wasn't alone.

"Is that Him?" A young boy who was maybe fifteen or sixteen asked with amazement.

"Who is this?" I asked impatiently.

"I'm Collin." He said seriously trying to stand taller. He was a lot smaller than Caleb, not so much in height, but more in mass. He looked scrawny compared to Caleb.

"My little brother, who is supposed to be home." Caleb said persistently.

"I'm a wolf too. I want to help."

"Exactly Collin, that's what I was talking about. You can't just start out with telling everyone that you are a wolf."

"He's an Angel..."

"Nephilim." Caleb cut in.

"... Either way he already knows. Someone's in trouble I want to help. No one does anything but hide now. I want to do something. Just because Ulric doesn't want us...

"You have to listen to Ulric and you know it." Caleb said

"But you don't. You broke away. I could too. We could be our own pack."

"Enough." Caleb growled. Instantly Collin seemed to obey. He clenched his jaw.

"I don't want to follow Ulric. I want to follow my brother."

Something about Collin reminded me of myself.

"So Liam, what's the plan? Are your Angels friends going to get Alana?"

"Not exactly." I hissed.

Chapter 22

Alana

Someone was pacing around me. I started to be able to lift my head and my eyes began to open. It didn't help much because it was mostly dark. "I have to find him, where would he have gone?" A deep voice threatened me. Although I wasn't sure if it was a threat or concern. I couldn't tell much about him. He was tall and very muscular. He just looked large. Period. The door opened and slammed. A dark heavy feeling came over me. The man was even larger than the first with black pants and tattoos covering his body. He wasn't wearing a shirt. He turned to look towards me and stared into my eyes.

"He will come for her." He said to the other men, and turned around.

It was as if he was intentionally showing me his back. At first I wasn't sure what I was looking at. It was a maze of tattoos and scars. In long stretches down his back near his shoulder blades ran two large, gruesome scars. But the scars became apart of the tattoos. Not like the tattoos were covering the scars, more like they were a part of them, embellishing them. They looked like something had been ripped and peeled away. 'His wings' I thought in terror. The two scars formed a tree trunk, from the tree truck there were branches. More than I could count. Although, instead of the tree having roots it seemed to have a mirrored imagine of an upside down tree with similar branches. Although, instead of leaves that covered the top, the bottom branches seemed to form daggers. It was like the top of the tree was being choked out by the bottom. The branches spread throughout his whole body. He walked so slowly and so confidently. He didn't say anything, neither did the other man. As much as I didn't want them to say anything, the silence was even more terrifying.

I heard coughing and heavy breathing. Had there been someone else in here the whole time?

"Liam?" I called out.

"What did you do?" The man yelled. His voice seemed familiar, but I didn't know where to place him. He was behind me so I couldn't see him. The man with the tattoos began to drag a chair in front of me with someone else tied to it. He looked so familiar, but I wasn't sure where I knew him from.

"Good now you too can meet." The man with the tattoos said.

"Laney are you okay?" The man in the chair said painfully. He looked like he had been beaten up severely.

Did he just call me Laney?

"Bastlon, if he does come we want to be ready. Let me go look for him." The first man said.

"Oh my dear Abner, faithfully ready to serve are you?"

Chapter 23

LIAM

"So just the three of us?" Colling said eagerly.

"You're not going, but I might know a few people who can help." Caleb said.

I was hesitant to follow him. I didn't want to waste any time, but who knows where she was being held and what would be waiting for me. We got in his beat up pickup truck. I would have figured him for a fancy sports car. Caleb and Collin sat in the front, while I hopped in the back. I didn't mind. I like the feeling of wind hitting my face, and honestly I needed a break from Collins constant need to talk and ask questions like a three year old child.

I'm not sure how long we had been driving, nor did I realize how distracted I had been during the drive. What I could tell now was that it was getting dark. Caleb pulled into the clearing of a woodsy area. The roads were made of dirt and there were trailers scattered around. It looked like a small community. I had heard that most of the wolf packs that are left either live in seclusion or travel often to avoid too much attention. I'm guessing that they have not been here too long, but it seemed like they had put down enough roots to suggest maybe a year or two.

He cut the lights like he was trying to sneak up, but with the old truck and bumpy roads I'm not sure who he was trying to fool. I heard Caleb talking to Collin in hushed tones, but didn't bother to try to make out what was said. Collin jumped out first and slammed the door, then Caleb shut his door quietly, walked around the truck and slapped his brother on the back of the head.

"You should stay here." Caleb said as he started to walk away.

He smiled. "You know what, Collin why don't you get to know the young Nephilim."

I was going to interrupt but Collin cut in front of me just inches from my face, which felt slightly uncomfortable, and then he began asking question. He was fascinated by wings and flying, wanted to know if we ate or slept, and what we did in our 'spare time'. I didn't really have any answers for him. I wanted to know what Caleb was doing and what was taking so long. I was ready to leave the both of them when I heard a fight break out. I blinked to where the noise was careful to stay out of sight and remain in angel form. I could tell that I missed something big.

"Get out of here and don't come back. You take your pack with you, but don't bother coming back. I'm glad Rule isn't here to see you!" Shouted the pack leader. He was in his mid-forties, but had an athletic build. He had the same dark eyes and soft dark hair as Caleb. "And take your demon with you! I can sense him hiding here. We won't break any accords we just want to be left in peace. If you ever try to come back, we won't be here."

Caleb looked like fire was going to shoot from his soul. From across the lot Collin looked scared, sad even. There were three others that followed Caleb. Everyone, including Collin, seemed to know what happened except me. I wasn't sure if I needed to know, but I couldn't help wondering. I had transformed back to my human self. Caleb and the two others walked right passed me. Caleb and Collin got in the front of the truck and the two other wolf people hopped in the back. There were no words, just silence. I hopped in the back as far from the others as I could. I just watched them to try to assess the situation.

It was a full moon so I knew they would start to change soon. Caleb pulled off to a secluded area. It was miles away from anything. Still, no one was talking.

"Caleb, we have to find her now. We don't have time to…" I was interrupted.

"To what exactly? To turn? Because we don't seem to have a choice. That was the deal our ancestors made. That's what your God did to us."

"That's what you asked for! You asked to be like me, but you're not! You were human! And you don't even know how good you had it."

"Good? Again, I didn't choose this. My ancestors did. Second. Ahhh..." He bent over in pain. I had never witnessed a werewolf change before, but it's not anything like I would have imagined. In an instant all five of them were screaming in pain as skin was being torn apart, bones were braking, teeth and nails began to get longer. It was so much bloodier than I would have thought. I honestly just wanted to do something to help them. I also knew werewolves could do a lot of damage to an angel, so I kept my hands near my weapons. Most clans have learned to control their blood lust, but there was always a chance of the animal taking over.

When the transition seemed complete it got eerily quiet. They all just stared at Caleb. Caleb Howled and took off. The others followed. At first I wanted to follow them, but there's no telling where those stupid dogs were going. Instead I went to search for Alana.

After a night of looking and 'asking roughly', I still had nothing. At about 5 A.M. I went back to the truck where the wolves had left last night. They are returning. They began to transition back into humans. It took longer than I really had the patience for. Finally Caleb walked up to me.

"So." I said.

"I know where they are keeping her." Caleb said.

Chapter 24

ALANA

We were alone again. It was just me and the beaten up man who sat across the room in chains. I could tell that even though he was in pain he was trying to keep his composure. It felt like he was trying to protect me, like Liam had. I studied the man, but it was hard to make out features. His body was covered in cuts and bruises and most of his face was swollen. It looks like he had been tortured. There was something familiar about him. Not just about the way he looked, but it was the way he felt. Or, better yet, the way I felt when I was around him.

My senses were scattered. I felt terrified, yet there was a blanket of comfort in the air. That wasn't all, I couldn't help but to also feel an overwhelming sense of curiosity. As much as I wanted to escape and be safe, I wanted to know who these people were and what was happening. Why me?

The man across the room had been mostly quiet.

There were a million questions I wanted to ask. I wanted to ask if the man was alright, how long he had been here, where were we, who were the people that took us, why had they taken us, but when I opened my mouth one thing came out. "What will they do if they find Liam?'

He didn't answer.

I could tell the man knew Liam, more than that, I knew he cared for him. He could maybe be his dad, but they looked to be close in age. He couldn't be more than a few years older than Liam. He seemed stiff, military like, except he kept looking at me with so much concern.

"Alana, Listen to me. We will get you out of here, they are just using you… Just do as they say and you will be okay."

His voice seemed so familiar. I know that I have met him before. If I could just see his face clearly I would remember him.

"You're like Liam, aren't you…? An Angel?"

Again, he didn't answer. Instead I was confusion and worry in his eyes. Clearly it was something that I was not supposed to know about.

I wanted to ask questions. I wanted to know more, but all I could think about was Liam. I'm here tied to a chair in a dark room with a man who looks like he has been tortured and people who… well don't seem to even be people, and all I can do is worry about him. A month ago all I had to worry about was midterms, but it's like there was a whole new world that I stumbled into like I was Alice in Wonderland. Like I had been blind this whole time.

There was a loud noise that started a commotion outside. It was hard to make out what was happening. I heard guards whispering and feet scampering around but I couldn't make out any words. I didn't know what was happening outside of these walls. Then one thing came to mind.

Liam? Instead of feeling comfort in the fact that he must have come to rescue me, all I felt was terror for him. So stupid. He has to know it's a trap. Maybe he wasn't alone. If there were more people like him, couldn't they have come too?

Chapter 25

LIAM

I guess the wolves got the scent of Alana last night. We started driving. My patience was running out. We pulled up to one of the old warehouses on the corner of the town. Surely this wasn't it. Wouldn't they be keeping her somewhere more secluded? This was a working warehouse. But then again, how better to hide than in plain sight?

"Alright, let's find an entrance."

"Liam. We have to be smart. There's at least ten guys out guarding entrances, and who knows how many are on the inside. We need a plan." Caleb said.

"I need to protect Alana."

"And how do you plan on doing that?"

"Caleb's right. You'd be an idiot to walk right in there." One of the other wolves said.

"Conner." Caleb said firmly.

"You can do whatever you want. If she's in there, I'm going to get her." I declared.

"And I'm coming with you." Caleb said.

"Then so are we." Collin and Conner said in almost unison. The other wolf just nodded in affirmation.

"No. Caleb and I will find an entrance and SNEAK in. Conner and Macon..." He seemed like he didn't want to give the order he was about to give. "We need you two to cause a distraction out front. Make sure the outside guards are looking at you so we can sneak by. Since you're wolves, and out of territory, that shouldn't be too hard."

"What then? That's it. What about me?" Collin pleaded.

"You need to go back to the pack. And that's final."

Collin didn't say anything. Not with his mouth anyways. His eyes were a different story.

No one else argued. If they were going to have any chance of defending themselves they would have to wait until dark when the moon came out. If it had not been a full moon, they would not be able to turn at all.

We spread out to keep watch to try to keep track of how many were there. Men came in and out, but we still had no idea of how many were in there to begin with. Nor did we know how many were humans, and how many were demons. Not from this far away. We could only assume vampires were waiting inside as well.

Caleb, Conner, and Macon barely made an effort to talk. Collin, on the other hand, it was hard to focus with him. There was something about him though. Maybe it was the idea of having a brother. I never had a family. The Angels were almost family, but none of them felt like brothers. Maybe Atticus, but he was more like a step-father. I hadn't thought much about him in a while and I started to feel sick with worry. I guess that's why Caleb was so hard on Collin. He worried. I don't know much about their pact but from what I've pieced together so far, they were all that each other had.

Finally, dusk began to creep up. Timing would soon be perfect to sneak in. Connor and Macon nodded at each other. They walked off so that they could be easily spotted by the guards.

"That's our que."

I nodded and took towards the entrance trying to stay in the trees, and then again in the mess of cars.

"Hey! Stop. What are you doing here?"

At first I thought they saw us, but they were yelling at the wolves. They were distracted. I couldn't tell, but I think Connor and Macon were fighting. I hoped it was a part of the plan. I didn't stick around to find out.

We slipped through the entrance. I kept my eye on Caleb, because I knew he would wolf-out soon. I didn't want it to cause a distraction. But then again, that would take their eyes off of me and I could find Alana and get her out. We slipped into a dark room. It looked like an office. A dirty office, but still an office. It astounded me to think of demons having a nine to five job. Like, I work at a plant shipping equipment on week days, but on the weekends I hunt people, drink blood, and damn souls to Hell? "Abner! Your orders are to stay here, or have you forgotten?"

Abner?! He's here? He has her? Rage filled me to the core.

I stood up quickly, but Caleb grabbed my shoulder and tried to pull me back down. I shrugged him off. He winced in pain and tensed his whole body. It was starting.

I left Caleb behind and peaked out into the hallway. Abner was Alone. It was weird to see him. I have heard about him, but they try not to talk about him. I've never seen a picture of him, but I knew who he was. He looked like me. I didn't like that. I didn't want to walk around with the same chin, the same mouth, the same shoulders as that… that. Monster.

I pulled my sword out and swiftly snuck out of the dark room. I slid up from behind him, pushed his back to the wall, and held him there with my sword to his throat. He didn't seem afraid. Instead he stayed calm and motionless. We stood there eye to eye.

"You don't want to make a scene Liam." He said quietly.

"Take me to Alana."

"It wasn't wise to come here." He said sternly.

"Wise? You want to talk to me about wise? Take me to her or I will slit your throat where we stand."

I heard Caleb scream in pain and loud noises from him knocking things over. I glanced back for a second before I left him grab my dagger from my belt and knock me in the head. It took me off guard and I fell back. I started to race toward him but Caleb busted down the door.

I kept my eyes fixed on him as he breathed heavily, ready to pounce. I kept my sword down, but gripped tight and ready.

'She's close." He said in a raspy voice.

I kept my eyes peeled on him as I stepped over to the dagger that Abner had dropped as he slipped away. I kneeled down to pick it up, all the while not taking my eyes off of Caleb. I nodded as if ready to follow him. He was fast, but swift. I was surprised at how little noise he made while sweeping down the hallways. We encountered a few Demons on guard, but before I could even leap towards them, Caleb had slaughtered them. Their bodies laid there with blood soaked rips and gashes.

Caleb kept going. We finally reached a locked door. He busted through the door, but backed up slowly. My heart sank and trembled with fear. Surely he would rush in after her if she were still alive. I could barely make my legs move. I pushed myself to enter the room. It was dark.

It only took a second for my eyes to adjust to the dimness of the room.

"Liam?" It was her voice. I ran up to her. She was tied to a chair I used my dagger to cut the ropes. She threw her arms around me and held me close.

"Are you okay?" She asked quietly, but with desperation.

I wanted to laugh. Was I okay? I pulled her hair out of her face and checked every inch of her face, then arms, and legs, and looked back at her face. Her hair was in a tangled mess and her clothes were dirty, but she seemed fine. I took her face in my hands and kissed her passionately. I moved my hands to the back of her head then down to her back holding her in a close embrace as our lips intertwined.

"Ehhm ehmm." A coughing noise came from the corner. I grabbed my sword until I realized it was Atticus. I was relieved to see him until I realized the torture he seemed to have endured. I tried to keep Alana close while I untied Atticus and checked him over to see if he was okay. All of the sudden I remembered Caleb was still waiting at the door. I assume that he was afraid of scaring Alana. I helped Atticus up and helped him as he limped towards the door. Alana was on the other side helping him. I don't know what Atticus had told Alana, but she seemed at ease with him. That is until she saw the man-like monster at the door. She glanced at me with fear in her eyes. I just nodded at her to assure her that he was safe. She stopped and looked into the wolves eyes. She seemed to study them, recognize them even. She looked at me with questions in her eyes.

Chapter 26

Alana and Liam

I was terrified, but I didn't want to show it. It helped knowing Liam was here. I wasn't sure if it was because I suspected he was more powerful than most people, or just because it was Liam. I couldn't take my eyes off of him. That is except to stare at the creature next to him. It seemed to be shaped like a man, but it had a wolf-like face, hair all over his body. He was taller than Liam was and had sharp claws on his hands, but he stood upright. He looked at me. He looked concerned for me. As I looked into his eyes I felt like I knew him.

I have begun to grow tired of being in the dark. I wanted answers, but I knew now was not the best time to sit and listen to fairytales. First we needed to get out safety. He man that Liam and I were trying to help began to stand a little taller.

"Are you crazy Liam?" He shouted. I could tell he was referring to the creature.

"He's on our side. It's the only way I could find her. To find you!" Liam said.

"He's here. Atticus. Abner is here. He's been this close the entre time and you never told me."

"It was none of your concern." The man he called Atticus explained.

I told Liam that we need to leave, that whatever it is can wait. It seemed to upset him, but then his face turned gentle again.

"Stay close to me." He whispered as he held my hand and brought it to his warm lips to an embrace. Even in this moment I wanted to melt. It felt like steam rising in me. I gulped and took a deep breath to steady myself.

"Always." I replied.

"How sweet." And unfamiliar voice stepped in.

^^^

"Baron, what are you doing here?"

He had his sword in his hand pointed towards us. I pulled Alana behind me, Atticus drug her further back and Caleb stood ready to pounce.

"I hear you met your dear old dad." Hearing him call him that made my stomach churn. Hearing him say anything my insides burn. This whole time he had been working with Him, my father. How long had he been working with them?

Another presence entered the room. Caleb went to attack, but Atticus held him back.

"Baron, put the sword down. We can talk this out." It was Idris. She must have followed us here. I kept my eyes on Baron, I wasn't sure I wanted to turn to face her just yet.

"Well this isn't fair, five against one". Five? Surely he didn't mean Alana. I turned to look back and Justin was there.

"Macon and Conner?" Caleb asked in his still unfamiliar voice.

"The wolves? They are okay for now." Justin replied assuredly with a nod.

"Atticus. Take Alana and get her out of her. Get her to safety." I said firmly.

Atticus slowly looked at Idris with question. She gave a nod signaling that that was her wish as well. Then she glared at me, which I only saw out of the corner of my eye because I kept a steadfast stare on Baron.

^^^

"I'm not going anywhere without Liam!" I shouted. Atticus was strong and tried holding me back. I could tell he tried to do so without hurting me. "This is a trap Abner and…. And the other guy are after him. Liam you need to leave." I pleaded

"Atticus!" Liam yelled.

I tried to duck under his arms but he wrapped his arms around me. It seemed like his arms could wrap around me twice. His grip was so tight, but so gentle. The creature growled at Atticus. I tried to jump up and kick, but the woman walked towards me. She brushed my hair back and everything faded away.

^^^

Atticus carried Alana away. It hurt to watch her leave, but my attention went back to Baron. I started to charge him.

"Liam. Wait." Idris said firmly. I stopped and inch from Baron who seemed to tremble. "We stick with protocol."

We tried sneaking out of the warehouse, even though the accords have obviously been broken. As much as I hated it, we were bringing Baron back to the sanctuary for trial. I also hated leaving Abner behind. He deserved to die, and if he stood in our way I would be the one to take him down.

Chapter 27

LIAM

We made it through the doors with minimal disturbances in which Caleb took care of. I was glad Alana was not here to see it. The other two wolves met us and seemed to await further orders.

"Idris. Fancy seeing you here. Although, I don't remember sending and invitation." I heard from behind me.

"Bastion. The accords have already been broken. You were harboring an innocent, a Guardian, and a trader we are taking them all back to our sanctuary now. We apologize for any bloodshed today and will meet to strike a new accords as to your convenience." Idris said firmly and calmly.

"Oh, but it was you who broke the accords. Well, your boy did. And honestly, I'm not sure I liked the rules anyways. You're not taking them anywhere. We want the girl back, your 'traitor', and we will be keeping the prisoner. And the boy stays too."

"Bastion. Let them go." Abner walked out of the shadows and said.

"Getting sentimental are we? I mean, that is your son. It seems the apple doesn't fall too far from the tree does it? I'm sure he would make a great contributor to my ranks, don't you think. A father son duo." Bastion said.

Idris warned me to stay close. By now we had Idris, Justin, Caleb, Connor, and Macon. All the while, they had an army of demons and vampires ranging from about forty to fifty in numbers.

"You aren't taking Liam he is one of ours." Idris said. It was the first time I heard her voice seem to brake. She cleared her throat and tried to remain composed. At that moment I felt how much she cared for me. Not just as a member of her Guard, but as a son perhaps.

"We don't need him." Abner seemed to plead. He stepped forward. "Idris, remember your promise." He said then pulled his sword. He looked at me with sorrowful eyes then let out a loud grunt and dropped his sword. Bastion had plunged his sword into Abner's back and pulled it back out. Abner fell to his knees still staring into my eyes.

I don't know what came over me. In that moment everything seemed to stand still. Time seemed to stop. All I could see was my father standing just a few yards in front of me bleeding out. I blinked my eyes, I tried to compose myself, to make since of what was happening. The, I saw Bastion swing his sword across Abner's shoulders. His head fell from his and rolled away from his body which finally fell forward with blood shooting out. Anger filled me as I started to charge, but before I could Idris took off after Bastion.

It was war.

They came at us, and we charged towards them.

Baron tried to ready his bow but I charged at him with my broad sword. He stepped back and began to flee. I was attacked by a crowd of vampires. Out of the corner of my eye I saw Idris on higher ground battling Bastion. There was an intensity in her that I had never seen before. I tried to keep my eyes open to focus on what was going on around me, but I also kept searching for Justin and the wolves. One after another I was attacked. There was so much going on that it was hard to sense those around me.

I turned back just in time to see Idris stabbed in the chest by Bastion. I wasn't the only one who saw it. A wolf who I didn't recognize jumped in to attack Bastion but was shot down by an arrow from Baron. I heard Caleb cry out in pain, but it wasn't his pain it was a pain of fear. I saw it then. It wasn't a wolf. It was a cub. Collin. My heart sank into my stomach.

Justin flew in with all of his might and knocked Bastion down. He wrestled him to the ground and punched him with his oversized hands. He grabbed his sword with both hands and plunged it into Bastions chest. Justin sat there for a second as if he was in shock. Him taking down their leader meant nothing to his followers they kept on at full force. Suddenly, Justin ran back to Idris who was still alive, but barely. Macon and Connor were holding back and slaughtering most of the small army. I flew over to Idris. She whispered something to Justin and he nodded and slowly backed away. He seemed to come to and ran towards the wolves to defend them.

I slumped down on my knees next to Idris, my leader, the woman who raised me and protected me always. I felt so helpless. I tried to heal her, but she grabbed my hand and told me to stop. She placed her hand on my head and everything started to fade away. I felt… out of body. Then I saw flashes of lights and heard voices. Images started to flood in, it was like watching a movie, but instead I was living it. It was as if I was fighting Abner. Wait no, not fighting training. It was a strange feeling, like we were close. More than close. I felt love for him. A secret love. Different flashes kept appearing before me. Abner smiling at me, at her. She liked the way it felt. She liked him. Liked him the way I like Alana.

She began to follow him. She was watching him with a woman. With my mother. A sense of jealousy rose in me. I could feel everything that Idris had felt. Then I was guided to a conversation. It was between her and Abner. Abner was begging for her to take in his child. Me. He made her promise to protect me. She begged him to tell her why he had done it. She felt terror because she knew what she had to do to him. He just wanted her to understand.

"Look within me, please old friend." Abner pleaded.

I saw her place her hands on his head. A new rush of images and emotions flooded in. It felt like a train switching tracks. More like a train running into me. Then images of a beautiful woman flooded through my head. Her smile, her eyes, her laugh. It was my mom. He hadn't rapped her, he loved her. Images of them together came faster and faster, leading to them kissing, then the feeling he got when she told him she was excepting a baby. He.... Was so overjoyed. And terrified, but terrified for her and the baby, not for himself. He wanted to protect her. I saw him taking her to the house where I kept Alana. He picked her flowers and brought her food. They were so happy.

Then I saw dark images of demons coming and attacking. He then surveyed the room and saw the once beautiful sanctuary windows were shattered and the flowers covered in the blood of the fallen and Catherine. He came to her aid and had no choice but to deliver the baby. As he tore through her once precious skin, he had a feeling the baby couldn't had survived this attack. As Catherine lie there howling in pain, Abner pushed through the agony knowing that he was killing her. He pressed on and eventually brought a healthy baby Nephilim boy into this dark world. But Abner had no time to rejoice, he knew this innocent child would be in danger and he knew this was all his doing. "What is it?" Catherine asked. Abner couldn't keep the warm tears in any longer, "A...boy, Cat." He paused to catch his breath.

"What do you-" he began. "Liam" she breathed. He saw her heart failing and her blood leaving her body. He looked around only to see he was covered in her blood. Just as she gazed upon her infant, her last breath left her body. He failed at protecting her life- one of the most precious things to him. Now he sat here, soaked in blood carrying a squalling baby.

The images stopped. I looked down at Idris. She was gone. I felt like I was gone. Everything I have ever known has been a lie. I felt hollow. I felt like a leaf that had died and was floating from its tree, its source of life. A pain filled my chest. I felt loss of a man that I have never known and a woman I have known my whole life. She loved him, that's why she protected me. I felt how hard it was for her to see him with someone else. I felt how heartbroken she was when she had to banish him. I felt his heartbreak over the loss of my mother. It was too much to bare. I screamed from the top of my lungs. I grabbed my dagger and slammed it into the ground.

Voices were fading everything sounded like it was in a tunnel. I was in shock. Then I heard Justin scream my name. I looked up just in time to see an arrow glide right past my head. I jumped up, but another one hit me in my shoulder. I still felt numb. I tried to pull the arrow out, but it was too deep. I broke off the access to give me range to move. I picked up my sword with my opposite hand and ran towards him. His sword met mine. I stared in his eyes and all the anger and furry seemed to want to pass through me.

I hadn't noticed but it was raining and lightning all around us. With it being dark, it made it hard to see. The moon and the lightning were lighting the scene. He swung at me, but I ducked. He lost his balance and I plunged my sword into his neck. I pulled the sword out and he fell to the ground. I still felt numb, but I also felt dizzy and weak. I dropped to my knees. I saw Justin look over with horror in his eyes. All of the demons and vampires were either dead or had fled. Caleb was with Collin who seemed to still be alive, barely. The sun was starting to come up and the wolves were all changing back. Justin started to run towards me but everything started to go black. I felt my head hit the hard ground. Then I felt nothing.

Chapter 28

LIAM

I tried to wake up but it was too bright to open my eyes. I stood up and felt dizzy. I wasn't sure how I had got here but I felt weightless. My memory started to come back. The pain everyone that I have lost came to my mind, but then a peace began to follow. I still could not open my eyes or see.

"Do not be afraid." A voice said, or was it voices. It sounded as if a choir of people were talking.

"Where am I? What Happened? Is Alana okay?" I pleaded.

"Be at peace. All will be answered."

"What does that mean?"

"Liam. You are not like most people, or angels even. You have the mortality of a human, but the power of an angel."

"Yes. I know that. I'm a Nephilim."

"You have been given a choice."

"Choice?"

"There are two parts of you. You have suffered greatly and a part of you has to die. Your decision you have to make is which part."

"Which part?"

"You may choice you be with Alana…"

"Yes!" I interrupted.

""You may choose to live as a human with Alana, but take caution. To live in the human world, you will desire the power you once had and the connection you have with the Father. The only way to ease the pain will be to remove your memories. The same will be with Alana. You will have every ability to be with each other, but the two of you will not remember each other and may never find a life together."

I stood frozen.

"You have another option. You are a great guardian and all you have ever wanted to do was please the Father. You are quite powerful, a good leader, and you have something most Guardians don't. You have experienced humanity. You may choose to take a position as a Guardian, but that will also mean not being with the human. Just as the other Angels and Guardians have. If you break a rule you are banished to the Fallen."

To be a guardian. That was all that I have ever wanted. But, now, had that changed? I have never wanted anything the way that I wanted Alana. But how could we be together if we didn't remember each other? They might still be after her and I wouldn't be able to protect her as a human. I wouldn't know her. As I thought about Alana, I also thought about how good it felt to be human. How it felt to experience the world.

"You do not have much time. You must decide."

I felt like two worlds were crashing. I wanted Alana to be happy. Either way they would take her memories of all things supernatural, all things me. My heart broken even more, as if there were no more pieces to brake.

I made my decision.

Chapter 29

ALANA

I felt cold and dehydrated. It was hard to swallow. I was laying on my back. I tried to open my eyes and sit up, but I felt very groggy.

"Laney!" I heard Lexi yell with excitement.

"Where..." I cleared my throat. "Where am I?"

"Hazel and Joe just left to get some food. Poor things they haven't eaten all day. I promised them I wouldn't leave your side. Laney honey, are you okay? You were in a car crash. Caleb was with you and brought you in. They said you are fine. No broken bones, you just bumped your head and were unconscious. We were so worried!"

"Caleb?" I still felt drowsy and confused. I couldn't remember anything.

"And Collin. They said they were giving you a ride and the car. Anyways, Collin... He's okay too but he got the worst of it. Apparently he wasn't wearing a seatbelt and went through the window. He's got some cuts and broken bones, but he will be okay." "Do you remember being in the car with Caleb?" Said asked slowly.

"Caleb?" "Yeah. I think so. I'm sorry, everything is just blurry right now."

"You know.... He hasn't left your side. Except to check on Collin." "Nor has he stopped talking about you." "I think maybe he feels guilty, or maybe he likes you." She said slowly.

"No, of course not. He's into you. You guys are a thing right? I've never even thought about him like that." I protested.

"I'm not sure he's my type. And plus, I don't like to be tied down." She said in a giggling voice.

I was able to go home the next day. Lexi and Caleb visited as soon as I got home. Grandma Hazel insisted I rest, but I wanted to be around people. I still felt confused about everything. I knew there were things I couldn't remember. I couldn't remember the crash or anything. Something felt different. Even Grandpa Joe seemed different. Perkier. Caleb seemed more worried about me than anyone. I wasn't sure why, but it seemed like he was keeping something from me. Maybe he felt guilty about the crash. I know he barely let Collin out of his sight, which wasn't a problem because Collin looked up to him. He followed him around like a puppy dog.

I tried to get back to normal. Caleb and I started spending a lot of time together. I knew it made Lexi happy. At first I felt kind of empty, like something was missing, but that feeling was replaced with a warm happiness. Although, there were times I felt like someone was watching me. For some reason, it didn't seem strange. It felt more like I had a new guardian Angel protecting me.

Chapter 30

Prologue

"Chief? Captain? All mighty leader?" Justin joked.

"Justin." I said sternly. He gave a small frown.

I knew that even though things were chaotic and solemn around here he was excited about my new leadership role. I wasn't excited. I was devastated and afraid, but in no way was I about to show it.

Months have passed since we lost Idris. I have been scrambling to reenact an accords and rebuild the leadership. Since being elected Head Guardian of our section, I took it upon myself to entrust Atticus as my second. I wanted to do things differently though. I decided it would be best if I stuck around as little as possible. Instead, I serve on a council. Mostly I travel. It helps to be far away from here, far away from her. At first I couldn't stop from checking in on her.

Caleb would sense me and at least be courteous enough to give me some space. The pain of jealousy arose in me every time I saw them together, and yet it gave me peace to know that she was happy. I knew that once things became serious between them he would have to reveal his… culture to her, which frightened me. Something within me know she could handle it though.

I tried to focus on other things.

For one, the retaliation from the Fallen in our region; which in turn lead to an uprising in surrounding regions. They were scrambling for a new leader, and there was talk of a secret weapon. I was on the search for whatever this weapon would be. That's when I found out it wasn't a what, but a who.

Printed in the United States
By Bookmasters